"Don't tell me you discovered love, Veronica,"

Jordan said lightly, although inside he was holding his breath for the answer.

"In a sense I did."

"Tell me about it," he replied with a touch of his typical imperiousness. He took her left hand and looked at the bare ring finger.

"No, I never married," she said in answer to his questioning look. "You and I used to say we wouldn't marry because our careers came first. And we started going out to protect each other from temptation, do you remember?"

"Lord, yes," he said with a grin, although he wondered what she would say if he told her that he'd suggested the arrangement because he'd been too shy to admit how much he really cared for her.

They wandered down toward the embankment and walked along the black, shining river. Jordan drew her close. "I want to make sure you're real, and you won't vanish like the other times," he said softly.

"The other times?"

"You'll probably think I'm crazy, but once or twice I thought I'd seen you, but when I turned, you'd be gone. I thought I was dreaming. But tonight," he added with a note in his voice that made her heart beat faster, "the dream became real."

Dear Reader:

The spirit of the Silhouette Romance Homecoming Celebration lives on as each month we bring you six books by continuing stars!

And we have a galaxy of stars planned for 1988. In the coming months, we're publishing romances by many of your favorite authors such as Annette Broadrick, Sondra Stanford and Brittany Young. And that's not all—during the summer, Diana Palmer presents her most engaging heroes and heroines in a trilogy that will be sure to capture your heart!

Your response to these authors and other authors of Silhouette Romances has served as a touchstone for us, and we're pleased to bring you more books with Silhouette's distinctive medley of charm, wit and—above all—romance.

I hope you enjoy this book and the many stories to come. Come home to romance—for always!

Sincerely,

Tara Hughes
Senior Editor
Silhouette Books

LUCY GORDON

A Night of Passion

Published by Silhouette Books New York
America's Publisher of Contemporary Romance

SILHOUETTE BOOKS
300 E. 42nd St., New York, N.Y. 10017

Copyright © 1988 by Lucy Gordon

All rights reserved. Except for use in any review, the reproduction or utilization of this work in whole or in part in any form by any electronic, mechanical or other means, now known or hereafter invented, including xerography, photocopying and recording, or in any information storage or retrieval system, is forbidden without the permission of Silhouette Books, 300 E. 42nd St., New York, N.Y. 10017

ISBN: 0-373-08596-6

First Silhouette Books printing August 1988

All the characters in this book are fictitious. Any resemblance to actual persons, living or dead, is purely coincidental.

®: Trademark used under license and registered in the United States Patent and Trademark Office and in other countries.

Printed in the U.S.A.

Books by Lucy Gordon

Silhouette Romance

The Carrister Pride #306
Island of Dreams #353
Virtue and Vice #390
Once Upon a Time #420
A Pearl Beyond Price #503
Golden Boy #524
A Night of Passion #596

Silhouette Special Edition

Legacy of Fire #148
Enchantment in Venice #185

Silhouette Desire

Take All Myself #164
The Judgement of Paris #179
A Coldhearted Man #245
My Only Love, My Only Hate #317
A Fragile Beauty #333
Just Good Friends #363
Eagle's Prey #380
For Love Alone #416

LUCY GORDON

is English but is married to a Venetian. They met in Venice, fell in love the first evening and got engaged two days later. After fifteen years they're still happily married. For twelve years Lucy was a writer on an English women's magazine. She interviewed many of the world's most interesting men including Warren Beatty, Richard Chamberlain, Roger Moore, Sir Alec Guinness and Sir John Gielgud. She also has camped out with lions in Africa and has had many other unusual experiences which at times provide the backgrounds to her books.

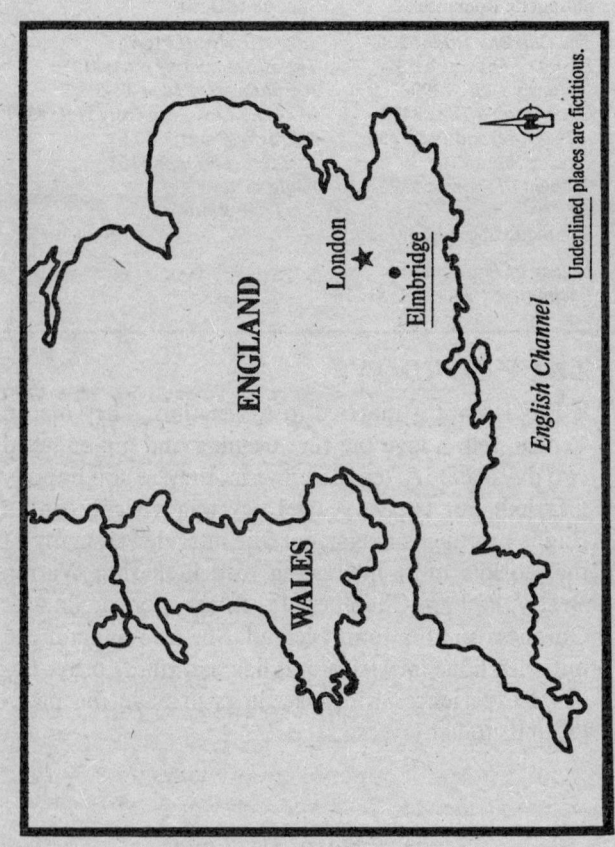

Chapter One

Veronica Grant crossed her fingers as she went through the entrance of the Clementine Model Agency. Jobs had been hard to get recently, and her need for a large sum of cash grew more urgent every day.

As she waited for Sally Clement, the owner and manager, to see her, she slipped a hand automatically into her purse and drew out a picture of her eight-year-old daughter, Holly. The photograph was several months old and showed a child who was small for her age, lean and wiry, with an expression full of energy and mischief. From the time she could walk Holly had bounced from one scrape to another, blithely indifferent to danger. She was sharp and intelligent beyond her years but with a sweet nature that prevented even her naughtiest pranks from being unkind.

Veronica's eyes stung as she realized how long it was since Holly had been well enough to misbehave. These days she had the heartbreaking docility of a child who was too tired for fun, and unless money could be provided for an operation she would continue to get worse. To her mother's frantic eyes she seemed to lose strength every day.

At first sight Veronica didn't look like the mother of an eight-year-old. She appeared younger than her twenty-seven years, with a mane of red-gold hair that tumbled gloriously around her shoulders and made a perfect halo for her heart-shaped face. Many women would have been glad of her flawless skin and sweetly curved mouth, but for as long as she could remember her alluring looks had been the bane of her existence.

Once she'd been a stagestruck and wildly idealistic adolescent, praying to be taken seriously as an actress. She'd dreamed of being willowy and mysterious, slaying theatrical critics with her haunting portrayals of Juliet and Ophelia. Instead she'd become a petite, curvaceous beauty with an open face, a voice that hovered on the edge of a chuckle and a body that might have been designed to show off a bikini.

At five foot three she had a tiny waist and high breasts, with hips that seemed made for jeans, turning male heads wherever she went. Instead of the great classical roles she was offered bit parts of scantily clad beauties in bedroom farces. She accepted them because she had to support Holly.

It was Sally Clement, a good friend, who had first suggested that she supplement her income with modeling. She was too small for the highest paid work, but she did reasonably well with bread-and-butter assignments. She modeled for mail order catalogs, perched on car hoods at motor shows and on yacht decks at boat shows.

As an actress, Veronica had learned to project the image that the photographers wanted—naive, zany, seductive, innocent or scatterbrained. She could widen her huge blue eyes to convey the essence of wonder, or look through half-lowered lids, hinting at tempting revelations awaiting the right man.

The one thing she never allowed to appear was her true personality, with its streak of fierce, independent pride that would have alarmed the marketing men. Her chin was dainty but it hinted at a stubbornness lurking beneath the surface. Her mouth was as sweet and curved as a baby's, and when she relaxed it in soft smiles for the camera, few could guess at her unyielding streak.

Only those closest to her knew her unbending nature, and she could remember a time when only pride and refusal to yield had enabled her to survive. Those qualities had carried her through the past few terrible months, when she'd discovered the seriousness of her daughter's condition. Now they enabled her to laugh and pose as if she hadn't a care in the world, while inwardly her terror was growing.

Her modeling assignments were no more artistically satisfying than her stage roles, but the money was better and she could spend her evenings at home with her daughter. Now she did only modeling and the occasional television commercial, but even so, she was far from amassing the sum she needed for Holly's operation.

But today Sally had called her with a hint of lucrative work. She'd been mysterious on the phone, refusing to spell out the details, and Veronica had hurried into the agency, full of hope.

Sally pulled open her door and hailed her friend. "Come in, Ronnie. Sit down." She cleared a space in her crowded office by shoving aside some papers on a chair. She was an attractive woman in her mid-thirties, with a kind heart, a sharp, humorous face and a no-nonsense air.

"You said you have something for me," Veronica said as soon as she was seated.

"Yes, I didn't want to tell you over the phone because it's not the kind of thing you usually do. It would mean posing naked—" Veronica groaned and Sally hurried on. "It's not porn, Ronnie. It's a series of ads for a new perfume called Jezebel. They promised everything would be tastefully done—and the caption would read, 'With Jezebel she's fully dressed.'"

Veronica's expression was wry. "What's the money like? That's the only question that really matters."

"It'll be a lot more than you've earned recently. I'll push it up as far as I can. I know how badly you need it." She looked at Veronica's tense expression and asked gently, "How is Holly these days?"

"She's no better, and she never will be until she has that operation." Veronica clenched her hands. "What breaks my heart is that she never complains. She's bored to tears with not being able to play games like other children, but she pretends she isn't because she doesn't want to worry me." She choked on the last few words and glanced quickly away.

Sally didn't try to speak words of comfort because she knew none could be offered to a woman watching her child slowly dying. She patted Veronica on the shoulder and concentrated on making coffee. When she'd set the cups down, Veronica had recovered and even managed an uncertain smile. "Does she know what's wrong with her?" Sally asked.

"She knows there's something wrong with her heart and that that's why she's always tired and breathless. I thought she might be too young to understand, but she's as bright as a button and she took it in." A desperate note came into Veronica's voice. "What I don't know how to explain to her is why she can't be made better."

"What about Derek? He's crazy about you. Can't he do anything to help?"

Veronica thought of the kindly, placid lawyer who wanted to marry her and shook her head with a rueful smile. "I need twenty thousand pounds, Sally. Derek has a good, solid practice, but I don't think he could raise that. I'd have some security for a loan if only I could have afforded to buy my own apartment, but sometimes it's hard enough just coming up with the rent. Oh, Sal, what am I going to do? Holly gets weaker every day, and I don't know how much more time there is left."

"Then it'll have to be Jezebel," Sally said. "If I can fix you up with a lucrative long-term contract, you'll be able to get a bank loan. There isn't another way of finding a sum like that." She laughed wryly. "Not unless you know a multimillionaire."

"As a matter of fact, I do," Veronica said slowly. "At least, I did once, only he wasn't a millionaire then." She went on, almost talking to herself. "Is it worse to swallow my pride or let myself be gawked at by strangers? I swore I'd die before I'd ask him for a penny, but Holly's all I have."

"This is like a riddle," Sally complained. "Question: Which man is such a swine that even his millions can't make him tolerable?"

"That's easy," Veronica said. "Holly's father."

Jordan Cavendish rubbed his hand over eyes that were beginning to sting. It was nine in the evening, and he'd spent the previous night on the Concorde doing paperwork. He tried to shrug his weariness away. Fortunately, he'd been born with the gift of energy, never needing more than four hours sleep a night. A punishing work schedule, plus financial genius and natural ruthlessness, had made him owner of Cavendish Holdings while still in his twenties. At thirty-three, he had a tall, muscular body that was kept hard and fit through workouts. He might have been a young athlete, except for his eyes, which were sharp and wary, the eyes of a much older man.

He picked up the microphone and began to dictate a memo to his chief executive. "I tracked down Aidan Wainright in New York and convinced him to sell me his shares, meaning I hold ninety percent of Wainright's and can legally compel Catterick to sell me his ten percent. Tell Catterick I'm tired of playing games, and he'll sell to me whether he likes it or not. I'll pay him the current market price, which is fivepence a share lower than my original offer. That's the cost of holding out on me. Memo ends."

He put down the microphone and rubbed his eyes again, wondering why he felt exhausted when he'd just pulled off a coup. He should have been high on adrenaline as he'd been so often in the past. Success—the knowledge that his employees stood in awe of him and his enemies feared him—that was the potent element that had sustained him since his first sharp deal. Tonight, for the first time, it had failed him.

The phone on his desk rang and he picked it up hurriedly. "I guessed I'd find you at the office," came Lorrayne's husky voice.

"Hell," he said impatiently, "I promised to call you as soon as I got back, didn't I?"

"I didn't expect you to keep *that* promise, darling—not unless you've changed."

Jordan grinned. That was the best thing about Lorrayne. After two lucrative divorces, she knew the rules and didn't demand more than he had to give. "Sorry," he said mechanically.

"I've got the champagne on ice."

He looked at his watch. "I'll be over in about an hour. I've brought you a present from New York."

"Mmm." Lorrayne's tone conveyed a precisely calculated mixture of gratitude and invitation. He'd heard it often before, but tonight it suddenly seemed as stale as everything else. "What is it?" she cooed.

He had no idea. His secretary had bought it. "Wait and see," he improvised hastily, and brought the conversation to an end before she could ask again.

After he'd hung up he pulled open a drawer and found the little wrapped package where Kate Adams always left the gifts she bought on his behalf. Beside it lay a bill from Tiffany's for a ruby bracelet. He whistled at the price, but he had no real complaints. He'd have been lost without Lorrayne. As a rich man Jordan had learned to cope with attempts to trap him into marriage, and even false paternity claims. Lorrayne acted as a protective shield but never made the mistake of trying to marry him.

He dictated two more memos, then took out a page proof of a newspaper article about himself. He'd given the interview on the strict understanding that he could veto it before it appeared. The editor had protested that it wasn't the paper's policy, but Jordan had stood firm. It wasn't *his* policy to become involved in anything he couldn't control.

The article was standard stuff: the shabby kid whose early years were spent in an institution in an obscure Midlands town; ambitious young financial wizard; worked night and day; lucky breaks; eye on the main chance; the first million, et cetera.

He noticed with satisfaction how much of the grim truth he'd managed to conceal. He'd spoken of the institution, but not the series of foster parents who'd returned him after a few weeks because he was 'unmanageable.' He hadn't mentioned his early feelings of possessiveness for his small items of personal property either—if there were no human beings he could call his own, material things had to take their place.

Nor had he tried to describe the day his lonely condition had ceased to be a burden and become a liberation, the day he'd realized that if he was no one's responsibility, he equally had no one to be responsible to. He'd been about fourteen when he'd discovered that heady freedom and known at once how valuable it would be in the years ahead. For he'd already marked out the path to the top of the world. And if the journey had been lonelier, crueller and involved more compromises than he'd expected, he'd made it nonetheless.

He grimaced as he came across the one personal detail he'd let slip. "The lean and hungry young man who ate hamburgers because they were cheap never forgot his dream of the champagne-and-oyster life."

Why had he told the journalist that? Perhaps because those days had been on his mind recently.

He'd been an apprentice accountant, handling the books of a small local theater. One of the actresses, as poor as he was, had shared his passion for hamburgers. They would meet in the local café and share a large burger between them, solemnly dividing the last sliver of onion into exactly equal parts.

Her name was Veronica, but she'd called herself Ronnie, as though by adopting a boy's name she could disguise her feminine curves and the slight huskiness of her voice. He'd gone half mad with wanting her, but he'd fought temptation, determined to steer clear of commitments. There'd been kisses, tormenting in their sweetness, but nothing more, except in his fevered dreams. He'd told himself he was respecting her youth, for she was only seventeen, but he'd known his innate caution had more to do with it. It was odd how shabby that had made him feel. But he'd soon pushed the feeling aside, as he pushed aside everything that threatened to distract him from his ambition.

Strangely, Ronnie had haunted his thoughts these past couple of weeks. Once or twice he'd even imagined he'd glimpsed her through the window of his car, but he'd told himself not to be fanciful—the past was just that. The picture with the article showed a man who was no longer "lean and hungry," but who radiated the assurance that only money and power could buy—a successful man who had everything he wanted.

Jordan made an uneasy movement, feeling a sudden need to get out into the cool air. He thrust everything back into his desk, pocketed the package with the ruby bracelet and stepped into the private elevator that went directly from his office to the garage.

But as he was about to open his car door he stopped. Or rather, something stopped him. The nostalgia that had troubled his ordered life recently, an ache for a more sweet and innocent past, was there again. But now it was overwhelmingly strong, resisting all his efforts to brush it aside. It whispered to him that there was a little place two blocks away that sold hamburgers.

Ridiculous! As though a man could recapture his lost self by a sentimental gesture. But even while the thought was passing through his head he'd pocketed the key and started to walk toward the exit.

He found the place easily. It was brightly lit, full of good smells and the cheerful sound of sizzling onions. There was an irrational lift to his heart as he walked up to the counter. "I want the biggest hamburger you have," he said.

Somewhere behind him the door opened and closed again, but he took no notice until he heard a woman's voice. It was musical and on the verge of laughter. "Don't forget my share of the onions."

He turned and found her standing there like a ghost he'd conjured up from his heart. She was a little older and a little more lovely.

"Ronnie," he breathed. He didn't know how he came to say the next words, only that they were true. "I knew you'd be here."

Chapter Two

"Ronnie," he repeated, impulsively seizing her hands, "It's so good to see you again."

"And you, Jordan," Veronica said, trying to clear her mind. She was thrown off balance by the warmth and fervor of his greeting. She'd thought he might not remember her, and had half expected him to smile with forced brightness and try to escape as soon as decently possible. Instead he'd greeted her warmly, looking down at her face with glowing eyes filled with an emotion she couldn't define.

There was a shattering moment when everything about him burned into her consciousness. She'd left an awkward youth and found in his place a man whose aura of power and virility seemed to fill the room. Something seemed to catch in her throat, and when she spoke again it was with difficulty. "It's been a long time."

"Nearly ten years. But I'd have known you anywhere. This is the most incredible coincidence—"

The man behind the counter interrupted with Jordan's hamburger. "I'll have another one," he said at once. "A large one with extra cheese and lots of onions." He raised a quizzical eyebrow at her to show he was reciting from memory. Veronica laughed, but his perfect recollection of her tastes added to her unease. When they'd been served Jordan ushered her to a table in the corner, where they sat looking at each other, then laughed self-consciously. "I can't believe this has happened," he said.

"But you said you knew I'd be here. I don't understand."

"I don't understand it myself. But I think my subconscious was hoping to see you again."

Now she recognized the strange emotion in his eyes. It was relief. For some reason Jordan had wanted to find her and had been frightened that he might not. Her heart sank. She'd planned this meeting with care, and now his spontaneous joy made her feel ugly and deceitful. But she thrust such thoughts away. She couldn't afford remorse. She was fighting for her child's life.

"Can you explain it to me, Ronnie?" Jordan went on. "You were always the one who understood mysterious things. I've been thinking of you recently, and suddenly, here you are, just the same as ever."

"After ten years?"

"You've hardly changed at all. You're just—" He tried to pinpoint the subtle difference that separated this poised woman from the unfinished girl he'd known. But his brain, so razor sharp where facts and figures were concerned, floundered at human complexity. "You're the same—only more so," he managed lamely.

"That's true of you, too," she said with a smile. "You've become what you once told me you wanted to be. I can't pick up a newspaper without reading about Jordan Cavendish the entrepreneur, the most feared man in the boardroom jungle."

He grimaced. "Can I help it if the gutter press talks nonsense?"

"Don't get embarrassed. You wanted to be feared, and to control a huge financial empire."

"I seem to remember you disapproved of my ambitions."

Her chuckle had the rich, delightful sound that had once made his head spin. "You never cared about my disapproval," she said. "And you were right. You've gotten everything you wanted."

For the second time that night the phrase made him uneasy. "Nobody gets *everything* he wants," he said quickly.

"You mean some brave soul's daring to hold out against you?"

"Let's leave the tycoon out of this. When we knew each other I was a starving apprentice accountant and you were a starving actress. We used to keep each other's spirits up. I was thinking of that only this evening. That's why I came here, and when you suddenly appeared it almost seemed like fate."

"Don't tell me you believe in such a nebulous thing as fate," she teased. "That would totally spoil my picture of you."

He reddened slightly. "I think tonight I could believe in anything." A smile transformed his expression. "If it is fate, I was never so glad of anything.

Ronnie..." He reached over the table and took her hand again.

It made her feel guilty to think how she'd studied him recently, seeking her moment. She'd read everything she could find in the newspapers and discovered that Jordan lived in jealously guarded privacy. He had no wife and seldom went out socially. On the rare occasions when he appeared in public he was usually accompanied by a dark-haired, sophisticated beauty called Lorrayne Haslam, whom the papers described as his "constant companion." As a prominent socialite Lorrayne was a minor celebrity herself. Veronica had seen her once on television and couldn't help but dislike her saccharine voice.

Calling Jordan's secretary for an appointment would have been impractical. She needed him to herself, with no fear of interruption, and for that she had to catch him off guard. She hadn't been able to discover where he lived, so she'd haunted his office building, noting his arrivals and departures. A couple of times, as he swept past her in his silver Rolls-Royce, his eyes had flickered in her direction, but abstractedly, as though he was looking through her. At last, tonight, he'd broken the pattern and walked. She'd followed at a discreet distance and had been able to slip into the shop behind him, as if by chance.

Now everything was going wrong. The young man she'd known years earlier had already begun to grow ruthless, and his recent career had seemed to prove that his heart had hardened even more with time. That was the man she'd tracked down and against whom she'd planned her strategy. But his joy at the sight of her had raised other memories of the raw sensitivity he'd concealed behind his brash self-confidence, the same sensitivity that had won her love.

"We talked about fate once," she said. "I said that if something was meant to happen, it would happen. And you called me a woolly-headed sentimentalist. You said you were going to take 'fate' in your hands and twist it into the shape you wanted. And you have."

He nodded. His will had been an anvil on which he'd beaten and hammered his life until it came out as he'd ordered. Now the sight of her caused an ache of loss in his heart.

"That was delicious," she said, finishing the hamburger.

Jordan immediately signaled to the counter. "I wasn't hinting for another," she protested as a second hamburger was set before her.

"It was how you hinted in the past," he reminded her, with a smile that held a touch of boyish mischief.

"So it was," she mused. It unnerved her further that the trivial detail gave him such pleasure. "And if we couldn't afford any more you'd cut off a piece of yours. You always gave me the lion's share."

"I think it was the only thing you were eating. You never stopped losing weight all the time I knew you."

At first she'd had traces of puppy fat, but after a few weeks her face had become more defined and her waist had whittled to almost nothing. For weeks he'd sat opposite her, just as he was now, enchanted by the loveliest features and figure he'd ever seen, desperately trying to imagine her without clothes.

With a self-conscious start he realized he was doing it again, but he couldn't help himself. She was a little thinner, with a touch of elegance that hadn't been there before. Her eyes, which had always been full of laughter, now had a sad, wary look that her bright smile couldn't conceal. He wondered what had happened to her, and he planned to have plenty of time to find out. She was warmth and light, and he'd lived too long without either of those things.

"Let's get out of here," he said when she'd finished eating. Once outside he slipped his arm around her shoulders. "Tell me about yourself," he said. "Are you still acting?"

"I do a bit, but I never became Juliet or Ophelia," she answered with a sigh. "I guess I just didn't have the talent. Now I do mostly photographic modeling."

"But you had such dreams," he remembered, "such ambitions."

"Yes, I did. But they all seem very far away now."

He looked at her curiously. "You don't sound as if you mind very much."

"I suppose I don't. Perhaps I just wasn't a very dedicated actress. Besides..."

She smiled, and there was something in her expression that made him ask jealously, "Have you found something that matters more?"

A vision of her daughter's face came into Veronica's mind: a little girl filled with personality, Jordan's child, yet not like him, except for an occasional wistful look in her eyes, as if she was trying to figure out the world. "Yes," she said softly, "I found something that matters much more."

"Don't tell me you discovered love?" he asked lightly, although inside, he was holding his breath for the answer.

"In a sense I did."

"Tell me about it," he said with a touch of his typical imperiousness. But Veronica only shook her head, and instinct warned him to go carefully. He took her left hand and looked at the bare wedding-ring finger. "No, I never married," she said in answer to his questioning look.

"I haven't either."

"I know," she said automatically, then caught herself up as he glanced at her with faint surprise. "I told you, the papers are filled with news about you," she said quickly. "We used to say we wouldn't marry, because our careers came first. We started going around together to 'protect each other from temptation.' Do you remember?"

"Lord, yes," he said with a grin, although he wondered what she would say if he told her that he'd suggested their mutual protection society because he'd been too shy to admit how much he really cared for her.

They wandered down toward the Embankment, and walked beside the black, shining river. The water glittered with reflected lights, and more lights were strung across the bridges like beads on threads. A cruiser went by, filled with laughing people. Jordan drew her close. "I want to be sure you're real, and you won't vanish like the other times," he said.

"The other times?"

"You'll probably think I'm crazy, but once or twice I imagined I'd seen you, but when I turned you'd be gone. I thought I was dreaming. But tonight," he added with a note in his voice that made her heart beat faster, "the dream became real."

So he'd noticed her following him after all, but hadn't understood. At least she could be honest with him about this. "Since I've been in this area recently, you probably really have seen me," she said. "There's no magic in that."

But he rejected the prosaic explanation that once he would have seized on. The hard shell that had encased his heart for years was beginning to crack, and he didn't want to stop it. Fate had given him a second chance, and he was shaken by a terrible need to believe that there could still be love and beauty in his life. "*I* think it's magic," he insisted.

"Jordan, what's happened to you? At one time you'd have been only too glad to believe in natural causes."

"Then it's time I changed. Too much realism is bad for a man." He pulled her into the shadow of the trees. "I need a little magic," he said softly, "and you were the only magic I ever knew. When you went away, the magic went with you." He felt giddy with the onrush of emotion, and before he knew it he'd brought his lips to hers.

Veronica stood quite still, astounded at the sensation of being swept along in a torrent of feeling that was beyond her control. The touch of his lips made her heart begin to beat more strongly until she could feel the pounding throughout her whole body. He first kissed her as tentatively as a boy, waiting for her response, then growing more urgent as he felt her melt helplessly in his embrace. He tightened his arms possessively and the movements of his mouth told of his mounting passion.

Something cried in her mind that this wasn't what she'd meant to happen, and then she reached up to slip her arms around his neck and was kissing him eagerly in return. Everything about him that she'd loved long ago was still there. Time seemed to roll back and they were once more the boy and girl who'd clung together for support against the world. Now she understood how lonely she'd been without him, and how desperately glad she was to be in his arms again.

When he released her they stared at each other, both in a state of shock. "I've been waiting to kiss you again ever since the last time," Jordan said unsteadily, "and now I never want to stop. All this time there's been something missing in my life. I didn't know what it was, but all along it was you." He drew her back into his arms, kissing her passionately.

"Yes," she murmured. "Oh, Jordan, how could this happen so quickly?"

"Because it had to happen. That's why you came back to me tonight, why you walked into that café just when I was there. That's why you've haunted my thoughts recently. It was meant all along. It's all so simple."

"Jordan, it isn't really as simple as that," she began urgently.

"But it *is*, darling. The important things are always simple. We never really left each other—not in our hearts. Tell me you feel that, too."

"Oh, yes." She clasped him to her, feeling the joy well up inside. He was right. However their meeting had come about, now that they'd rediscovered each other it would be easy to tell him what she had to, and everything would work out for them.

Way above them, Big Ben struck. Jordan stiffened and looked at his watch. He was astounded at the time. He'd promised to be with Lorrayne ages ago, but Veronica had made him forget everything else. He could feel the weight of the bracelet in his pocket, reminding him of years of loveless kisses, carelessly given and lightly received. How different was this kiss with a woman who smelled of spring and wildflowers, that had rocked him to his very depths. He was happy for the first time in years. "To hell with the time. I've found you now and I won't let you leave me again."

"I—leave you? It was you who left me, Jordan."

"That's not how I remember it. Oh, what does it matter? We're together again. This time we'll make it perfect, sweetheart. Yes, I know—" he silenced her as she tried to speak "—I know I'm rushing you, but you remember how I am when I've decided on something."

"Yes, I remember," she said with a shaky laugh.

"And if we want each other... Darling, tell me I'm not fooling myself—"

"No, that is—" She drew away from him, dismayed by the headlong speed at which he was rushing her. "Jordan, there's something I've got to tell you. Let me take you home with me and...well, you'll see."

"All right, I'll come home with you." He took her face between his hands. "I'll go anywhere you lead me. In all my life, I think you're the only person I've ever really trusted." The words didn't begin to express his true meaning. He wished he had a subtle tongue to tell her that she'd caused a flowering in the desert where he'd lived until now. But there would be time, and somehow he would let her know, in actions if not in words.

They collected his car and he drove to the apartment block where she lived. In the elevator they held hands and smiled at each other, but now the moment had come Veronica's heart was beating with mingled apprehension and joy.

Once inside her apartment he tried to take her into his arms again, but she put him gently aside. "Wait here a moment," she said.

To his surprise she went out of the front door and he heard her taking the elevator to the floor above. He looked around him at her home. It was like her coat, he thought, serviceable but not good enough for her. He smiled as he thought of how he'd enjoy showering her with beautiful things.

He heard the elevator return and went to stand at the front door. The doors opened and he saw Veronica standing with a little girl, dressed in a robe and pajamas, who looked as if she'd recently awoken. She led the child into the apartment. "Jordan, this is my daughter."

Holly didn't smile, but she extended a hand to Jordan, studying him with an unwavering gaze.

"Hello," he said, shaking her hand. "I'm Jordan."

"I'm Holly. How do you do?"

He was charmed. Normally he felt awkward with children, but he was touched by this pixie's air of gravity, almost as though she wasn't a child at all but a wise old lady.

"Can I have a drink, Mommy?" she asked.

"Of course, darling. I'll make you some hot milk. Then it's time to go to bed." She turned to Jordan. "Holly stays with my neighbor upstairs when I have to be out."

Veronica went into the little kitchen, and Holly walked to the sofa and sat down. It seemed to Jordan that her movements were slow and oddly careful for a child, but he assumed she was still groggy. Despite her evident sleepiness her pale face was vivid with intelligence. He studied her features, trying to see a hint of her mother's beauty, but only Holly's curved mouth reminded him of Veronica.

Holly leaned over to a bookshelf by the sofa and took a paperback that she slipped hurriedly beneath her robe. Looking up, she found Jordan watching her, and put a finger to her lips. There was an almost adult twinkle in her eyes.

"It'll be our secret," he promised. "Are they all yours?" he asked, indicating the books. She nodded. "What do you like reading about?"

"Murder," Holly said. "Or spies. But I prefer murder, as long as it's a good one."

"What do you call a good one?" he asked cautiously.

"Nice and complicated. With some of them, you can tell whodunit in chapter two. What's the point of that?"

"No point at all," he agreed, obviously taken. Although he couldn't help but be surprised at such a small child's choice of reading.

"Here you are." Veronica returned from the kitchen with a mug of hot milk. Holly took it and reached up to kiss her mother. "And before you go," Veronica added, "I'll have whatever you're hiding in your robe."

With a sigh Holly pulled out the book and handed it to her mother. "Good night," she said to Jordan.

He grinned. "Good night. Perhaps you'll have better luck next time."

"No I won't. I never do," Holly complained. She cast her mother a dark look and sighed, "Honestly, sometimes it's like living with the CIA."

Jordan passed a hand tactfully over his mouth, and avoided Veronica's eyes until they were alone. "Does she really guess who the murderer is by chapter two?"

"Frequently. It's alarming how bright she is. She could read properly when she was four."

"She's a delightful child."

Veronica took a deep breath. "I'm glad you like her, Jordan. Because she's yours."

He frowned, hearing the words but not quite taking them in. "You mean," he said at last, "you want me to be a kind of father to her?"

"I mean you *are* her father."

Jordan didn't move. His only reaction was a slight narrowing of his eyes. "What are you talking about?"

"Holly is your daughter. She was born not long after we separated."

Jordan got up and looked at her. His blank eyes gave no hint of the numbing sense of disillusion that was taking hold of him. "You waited a long time to tell me I had a child," he said flatly.

"Too long. Oh, Jordan, I know that now. But there were reasons—"

"Yes, I can imagine," he broke in quietly. "I can also imagine the reasons for suddenly producing her now. I'm familiar with them all. In fact I'm familiar with this whole depressing, sordid situation."

Veronica caught her breath at the deadly contempt in his last words. She'd tried to hope that Jordan's quietness was merely due to astonishment, but there was no doubt of its menacing quality. "Jordan, I know what you must be thinking—"

He smiled coldly. "I don't think you do, Veronica. At least, I hope you don't. You wouldn't like what I'm thinking about you right now."

"At least listen to me—"

"But that's what I've been doing all evening, isn't it?" he reminded her gently. "You did a beautiful job, Veronica, I'll give you that. There aren't many people—men or women—who can say they took me for a sucker as completely as you did."

"How can you say that, Jordan?" she insisted.

"Come on, Veronica! Are you saying it was coincidence that we bumped into each other tonight?"

"No," she admitted. "I followed you into that place."

A mist seemed to clear in front of Jordan's eyes. "You followed me," he echoed. "You've been following me for days, haven't you? When I thought I saw you, I wasn't imagining things—you were really there."

"I had to find you alone. It was important. Please, Jordan—"

He was talking half to himself. "And tonight, when I went to the café, you were a few steps behind me. You waited until the right moment and then—" he drew in a sharp breath "—I walked right into your trap. You set me up for everything that happened tonight. You even gave me a clue when you said you'd been reading about me. You checked out how much I was worth before deciding whether I was the man to go after. You even checked out that I wasn't married. A wife would have got in the way of your devious little schemes—"

"No, it wasn't like that," she cried.

"But you've already admitted that it was. You've been trailing me for days, waiting for a moment when I was off guard and you could take me for everything you could get. But you miscalculated, Veronica. You should have picked a man you'd slept with."

"But we—"

"I never made love to you. Even after all this time I haven't forgotten that. You counted on my being hazy about it, but what you didn't know was that I used to be half demented from wanting you. I spent night and day thinking about how we'd be together. I dreamed about you when I should have been working."

"That's why you got rid of me, wasn't it?" she broke in bitterly. "I was in the way of something you wanted more."

He made a tired gesture. "What difference does it make now? We separated, and I *know* we never made love, because if we had—" He stopped. He wasn't going to admit to her that if they'd made love it would have been an earth-shattering event that he could never have forgotten.

He'd been virtually in a state of shock. Her bombshell had caught him unprepared and had blasted through him, tearing at feelings made vulnerable for the first time in years. The numbness that follows injury had briefly protected him, but now it was wearing off and he saw this woman, whom he'd almost been prepared to worship, revealed as a tawdry schemer. The bright dream that had enchanted him was a conjurer's trick, performed for money. Pain possessed him, so intense that it took his breath away, and he clutched the mantelpiece to steady himself.

"And now," he went on, "after all this time you produce a child who looks nothing like me, and claim she's mine. What kind of a fool did you think you were dealing with? Of all the clumsy, stupid—" He closed his eyes and his voice grew suddenly husky. *"Why did you have to do it?"*

Horrified, Veronica put out her hand, but before she could touch him, his face had hardened. When he opened his eyes the brief moment's weakness had vanished and she found herself looking into a face as hard as stone. "You won't get a penny out of me," Jordan declared flatly. "She's not my child and you know it as well as I do."

The sound of a door opening made them both turn. A man in his late thirties with a pleasant but slightly vapid face had emerged from Veronica's bedroom. "You're not going to escape your responsibilities that easily," he declared.

"Derek," Veronica whispered. "What are you doing here?"

"I came in case you needed help, and it's a good thing I did. You haven't made such a job of tackling him, so now you'd better leave it to me."

"My God, there's nothing you wouldn't stoop to!" Jordan flung coldly at Veronica. "You even had a witness, just in case I could be trapped into an admission."

"I didn't know Derek was here," she protested.

"Who let him in then, or did he walk through the wall? Never mind. Whatever you two had in mind, it's failed. If you try anything again, you'll be sorry."

"Not so fast." Derek had planted himself between Jordan and the door and put out a hand to restrain him. Jordan barely looked at him as he thrust him aside in one swift movement.

"Jordan, wait!" Veronica cried.

He turned at the front door. "Don't try to contact me again, Veronica. Don't write, don't call, don't do anything to remind me you're alive. For both our sakes, let me forget all this as soon as possible."

The last thing she saw was his face, filled with hatred, before he slammed the door.

Chapter Three

Kate Adams came out of Jordan Cavendish's office and closed the door quietly behind her. Brenda, the second secretary, looked up sympathetically. "He's no better, then?"

Kate sighed. She was a motherly woman in her fifties who survived in a demanding job by being as unimpressed by Jordan's rages as she was by his vibrant attractiveness. She was also efficiency personified, but even she had been going around on tiptoes recently. "He's worse," she confirmed gloomily. "*Vile* is the word that describes his temper, I think. Yes, definitely vile."

"It started just after he got back from New York on that Wainright business," Brenda recalled. "I thought you said it went well."

"It did. But you're right, he's been acting like a bear ever since."

Inside his office Jordan Cavendish knew his staff was discussing him, speculating. Let them speculate. None of them would come near the truth.

It shocked him to think how easily he'd been taken in. He could see now that his nostalgic mood that night had been caused by the brief glimpses of Veronica he'd had while she was following him. They'd roused his subconscious, causing it to dwell on the past. He cursed as he recalled how he'd thought their meeting was fate!

The rigid control Jordan had imposed on himself in Veronica's apartment had lasted all the way home. He'd told himself the business was over. But whenever he closed his eyes, her face was there, laughing, gentle and enchanting.

For a few hours he'd dreamed that the arid course of his life might yet be altered. But she'd planned it all, watching him every moment to see if her spell was taking effect. At the thought of some of the things he'd said to her, his control had finally broken and he'd slammed his hand down onto a small table so violently that its glass top smashed into tiny slivers.

Weeks had passed, but he hadn't escaped from his wilderness of pain and confusion. He was grieving, not just for his dead illusions, but for the loss of an old, sweet memory. He hadn't known how much that memory meant to him until it was destroyed.

Now, sitting in his perfectly ordered office, he came out of his reverie to realize that once again his mind was going around the old treadmill.

The light was poor. Earlier he'd drawn the blinds over his huge plate glass windows against the dazzling afternoon sun, but now the sun was close to setting. He strode to the windows and pulled on the cord, glancing briefly at the building across the street where some men were erecting a huge poster. Then he froze.

The last piece of the poster had just been pasted into position. It showed a naked woman reclining gracefully beneath the legend, "With Jezebel she's fully dressed." Her pose was delicate—almost modest. Only her smooth, beautiful buttocks were clearly revealed, then a turn of the body hid all but a hint of one full breast. Her face, framed by a glorious cloud of red-gold hair, had a softly provocative smile guaranteed to drive a man wild.

The sound of the blinds snapping against the window brought Jordan sharply back to himself. Tight lipped, he stared at Veronica's face, then at the lovely body he'd once yearned to possess and had never even seen. Both were now exhibited, naked and forty feet high, to any stranger who passed that way. He wanted to bellow his rage and anguish to the world.

But he controlled himself. Displays of feeling were for weaklings. What Jordan Cavendish did was act.

For the first time in months Veronica dared to let herself hope. The money for her first Jezebel advertisement had been good, and the firm had promised her a long-term contract if the initial response was favorable. Her bank manager had smiled and agreed that a contract could be security for a large loan.

The photographer was lyrical, swearing that these were the best pictures he'd ever taken. Sally called her to report that the firm's directors were thrilled with their impact. Holly was nearly safe.

She'd forgiven Derek for his ill-timed intervention on the night she'd told Jordan about his daughter. She'd been furious at the time, but in retrospect she'd admitted to herself that it had probably made little difference. Jordan had decided not to accept Holly and nothing would have changed his mind.

And perhaps it was better to make the money herself, even if it did mean allowing strangers to look at her in the nude. Derek had blanched a little when she'd told him, but then he'd immediately proposed again, to show it didn't make any difference. That was sweet and loyal of him, and she wished she could have said yes. Until recently she'd meant to, knowing that Derek was a kind and good man, but the memory of Jordan's kiss and her own shattering response was still vivid in her mind. Out of fairness to Derek she must exorcise that ghost before she came to any decision.

But Jordan's ghost wouldn't be exorcised. He haunted her, reminding her that she'd deceived him and inflicted a cruel wound. She wished she could blot out the memory of his face filled with disillusion, the telltale huskiness when he thought he understood what she'd done.

The fight for Holly's life had forced her to ignore everything else, but she would have liked to tell him that she was sorry for hurting him.

When she picked up the phone one morning to find Sally on the line, her heart began to beat with eager hope. But Sally's first words were, "Ronnie, I don't know how to tell you the bad news."

Veronica clenched her fingers on the receiver. "Go on."

"Jezebel won't be using you anymore. That whole advertising campaign has been vetoed from on high."

Despair washed over her in ugly waves. It couldn't happen, not when she'd been so close. "But how can they?" she managed to say in a shaking voice. "The managing director himself said he loved it, and sales went up at once."

"The managing director still loves it," Sally said, "but it's not his decision now. The firm's been taken over in the past few days, and apparently the first thing Jordan Cavendish did was to say you were out."

Veronica tightened her hand on the receiver. "Did you say Jordan Cavendish?"

"Jezebel has been swallowed up by Cavendish Holdings. I can't think why, because Cavendish has never shown any interest in cosmetics before."

"I can think why," Veronica whispered bitterly.

"What did you say?"

"Nothing," she said hastily. She'd told Sally she was going to approach Holly's father, but she hadn't mentioned Jordan's name. Now she was even more grateful she'd kept the secret. "Thanks for letting me know, Sally."

Veronica hung up and sat by the phone in a state of shock. She'd known Jordan could be ruthless, but she'd never dreamed he would go to these lengths for personal vengeance.

Suddenly she snatched up her purse and ran for the elevator. In the street she hailed a taxi and gave the driver the address of Jordan's office. She was going to see him, even if she had to mow down an army of secretaries with orders to keep her out. Despair had given way to a killing rage and she was as dangerous now as a tigress protecting a threatened cub.

At his office building she jumped out and ran straight past the reception desk. A wall board listed the offices, and she pressed the elevator bell for the fifth floor. Once in Jordan's outer office she headed straight for the door bearing his name. A gray-haired woman rose to intercept her, saying, "Can I have your name, please?"

Veronica rapped out her name and prepared for battle. But the woman merely opened Jordan's door and said, "She's here." Veronica heard Jordan give an order not to be disturbed, then she was in his office and Kate was discreetly closing the door behind her.

"I've been expecting you," Jordan said.

"You petty, vindictive bastard!" she flung at him.

He paled. "If we're going to call each other names, I could call you a few, couldn't I?"

"I've never done anything as low as throwing someone out of work just for spite. How long is it since you were poor, Jordan? Long enough for you to forget what it's like to be desperate?"

"You showed me how desperate you were a while ago," he reminded her coldly. "Desperate enough to lie."

"I never told you any lies—"

"Please, let's not go through all that again. You told me a pack of lies, and when that didn't work you paraded yourself for the world to see. Look—" he pointed her in the direction of the window facing the billboard, where two men were in the process of taking the poster down "—it would have been inconvenient to have to look at you every time I raised my head," he said coolly.

"So the mighty Jordan Cavendish used his millions to brush me aside. It must be wonderful to have such power and not need to spare a thought for the lives you're destroying."

"Let's not be melodramatic," he snapped. "It won't take you long to find another victim."

"The only victim is going to be Holly," she cried. "I could have saved her life with that money. But you don't give a damn about that, do you? After all, how much does a child's life weigh in the balance sheet? But I tell you, Jordan, if Holly dies because of you, I'll make you sorry you were ever born."

"What are you talking about?"

"I'm talking about *your* daughter, who's dying."

"Is this another of your tricks? She looked healthy enough." But he felt a moment's uncertainty as he remembered Holly's slow, unchildlike movements.

"She's got a serious heart condition, and it's slowly killing her," Veronica said emphatically. "She needs an operation, and we don't have medical insurance."

"For something like that you don't need insurance," Jordan said. "State medicine is excellent in emergencies."

"But Holly isn't classified as an emergency," Veronica said despairingly.

He stared. "That's impossible."

"It ought to be, but the doctor said the waiting lists were so long that an 'emergency' was someone who'd die tomorrow if they weren't treated today. He told me she could go on as she was for months before it became that urgent. It'll only count as an emergency when she collapses, but by then it could be too late.

"She's been waiting for six months. The doctor says there's still time as long as she takes it easy, but she's growing weaker, and she never seems to get further up the list. Her only hope is a private operation, but it'll take twenty thousand pounds."

Her voice broke on the last word, and she fought to control her emotion. So much depended on making him listen. When she'd mastered herself and looked up, Jordan had moved closer and was frowning at her. "So this is what it was all about," he said broodingly. "No wonder you went to any lengths to get money. But why didn't you just come to me straightforwardly? We were...fond of each other once, and you could have asked my help as an old friend. There was no need to set me up like that."

"I didn't set you up," she insisted.

"I'd say you set me up rather thoroughly, complete with a witness, from the press, I presume. Or was he a lawyer?"

"Derek does happen to be a lawyer, but our relationship is personal. And I told you I didn't know he was there."

"Nonsense. You must have let him in."

"I didn't. Derek has a key."

There was a silence. "I see. That kind of personal."

"It isn't what you think...at least...he wants to marry me, it's true. But he has a key because he sometimes comes in to look after Holly while I'm out. He's a kind man and she's very fond of him."

"And he's in love with you?"

"Yes."

"Then why didn't *he* get you the money?"

"He couldn't raise that much. Besides, he isn't Holly's father—you are."

"Then why didn't you come to me six months ago?"

"Much good it would have done me!" she flung at him. "At the time there seemed a good chance I could raise the money myself. I had two decent offers close together, but one fell through and one didn't pay as much as I'd hoped. I did everything I could think of before turning to you—"

"Thank you," he snapped. "I don't really think I deserved that, but it's academic now."

"I knew you'd be hard to convince. That's why I didn't come sooner. But I never thought you'd simply shut your ears and refuse to listen."

"You knew I'd be hard to convince," he echoed. "That's why you went through that little performance to soften me up. Get a man so dizzy with desire for you that he doesn't know whether he's coming or going and you can make him believe anything, including that he fathered a child with a woman he never made love to."

"But you did," Veronica said wildly.

He groaned, "Veronica, please, drop this. If we'd been together I'd have remembered."

"Not in the state you were in. It was during your exams. You had a terrible cold and you were sure you were doing badly. I managed to scrape together enough to buy half a bottle of whiskey, and dosed you with it. You drank it all very quickly and dozed off... and then..."

And then she'd taken him in her arms, trying to show the love she was afraid to speak. He'd rested his head on her breast, his eyes closed, and she'd kissed him tenderly again and again. She'd thought he was asleep, but gradually his grasp had grown more possessive, his touch more urgent. And she'd yielded to her overwhelming love for the first and last time.

Veronica looked up to find Jordan's eyes on her, and their blank, unyielding expression made her heart quail.

"And then?" he asked quietly.

"And then it happened," she finished tersely.

Jordan didn't speak, and it took all her courage to go on. "In the morning you didn't seem to remember and I couldn't bring myself to speak of it. Perhaps I should have told you then, but I felt so vulnerable when you didn't say anything." She sighed. "It's easy to be wise after the event."

"But when you found yourself pregnant you could have told me."

"How could I? You'd made it very clear you didn't want me. We agreed not to tie each other down, didn't we? If this hadn't happened I was never going to tell you about Holly at all. Jordan, it's the truth. I swear it. Surely you haven't forgotten how you were that night?"

"I remember the cold and the whiskey. It send me into a deep sleep, and when I awoke I felt a lot better. But as for anything else..." He made an indecisive gesture.

"We made love," she said urgently. "And Holly was conceived."

Her face was upturned to his in a look of entreaty. Jordan put out a hand to her but stopped himself at the last moment and turned sharply away. He went to the window and stood with his back to her, while confusion raged within him. It would be so easy to trust that candid face, those clear, beautiful eyes that seemed to reflect a soul incapable of deceit.

But she'd taken him in once before. She was a woman fighting for her child's life, which meant she acknowledged no rules. Fool! he thought, to be so easily deluded a second time. He felt the chill relief of a man who'd spotted the hidden trap in time.

Veronica had seen his slight movement toward her, the eagerness in his eyes, then the blankness as though he'd forcibly restrained himself. As he stood at the window she watched his back, holding her breath, praying. But she knew her prayers hadn't been answered when he lifted his head and set his shoulders decisively. It was the action of a man who'd come to a clear-headed decision, unswayed by emotion.

"Veronica," he said at last, turning to face her. "I'm going to offer you a bargain. I don't believe your story and I never will. Please understand that that's final. I want you to sign a legal document declaring that I'm not Holly's father and renouncing all possible claims on me."

"And why would I do that?" she demanded incredulously.

"Because if you do, I'll pay for Holly's treatment. You can have as much as you need, but I want your signature on that document."

She stared at him wildly, wondering how this could be happening. Her child's life in return for a monstrous lie. She turned away, running a hand distractedly through her hair. The movement gave her a view of the billboard, from which the last section of the poster had been removed. Her last hope, she realized with sickening despair, and he'd destroyed it as casually as he would swat a fly. There was nowhere else to go.

She turned back to face him. "Very well," she said bleakly.

"Don't say that without understanding what you're agreeing to. It means that the pretense that Holly's my daughter is over, that you agree the whole thing was an invention and promise never to repeat it."

"I'll sign anything you want," she whispered. "Only make her well again."

"Then let's get down to business," he said briskly. Waving her to a chair before his desk he seated himself and picked up a pencil. "Who's Holly's specialist?" he asked.

She told him the details and after jotting them down he flipped a switch on the intercom and gave Kate the name and number. It had once taken Veronica two days to be put through to the "great man," but Jordan reached him at once. Ten minutes later the operation had been booked for the following week. For Jordan Cavendish it was as simple as that.

"He'll do it in the Jameson private clinic," he said when he'd hung up. "It's a good place and you can be with her as much as you want. He says he doesn't anticipate any problems, and she should have a quick recovery."

"Thank you," Veronica said incredulously. "I don't know how—" She fought to control the tears that welled up, but she couldn't. She'd held out for six terrible months, but the strength that had sustained her vanished abruptly. She buried her face in her hands and sobbed her relief.

Jordan ground his nails into his palms. He wanted to take her in his arms and comfort her. He wanted to send her out of his life and never have to see her again. He didn't know what he wanted.

At last he said gruffly, "Come on, there's no need for that," and left his desk to cross to the liquor cabinet. After a few minutes she lifted her head and found herself looking at a glass of brandy. "Drink it," Jordan instructed.

She took a few swallows and felt better. While she drank the rest Jordan sat down at a typewriter, then rose a few minutes later with two typed sheets, which he pushed across to her. Each contained an identical declaration that Holly Grant, daughter of Veronica Grant, was not the child of Jordan Cavendish, and that Veronica Grant would make no attempt to claim otherwise.

"Is this all it is?" she asked, surprised.

"What were you expecting?"

"I don't know—a battery of lawyers, I suppose."

"I'd rather keep this between the two of us. Kate can witness our signatures, but even she doesn't have to see the contents."

She'd been dreading having to sign under the contemptuous eyes of Jordan's legal advisers, and she looked up to thank him for this unexpected consideration. But he'd already gone to the door to call his secretary. Kate Adams came in, and they both signed in front of her. Then Jordan drew a sheet of paper over both copies while Kate signed as witness.

When they were alone again he handed a copy to her. "We each have a copy," he said formally. "You have nothing further to worry about. The bills will be sent directly to me. In fact, there'll be no need for us to meet again. Now, if you'll excuse me—" He began ushering her toward the door.

"Jordan, wait, let me thank you—"

"You don't owe me any thanks," he said dismissively. "I'm just paying a debt long overdue."

"You are?"

"It was only with the help of your nursing, and your whiskey, that I got through my last exam. I owe you for that."

"But you paid me for the whiskey."

"What you gave me was worth far more. Passing those exams gave me what I wanted most in all the world."

"Then we're even, because Holly's health is what *I* want most in the world."

Her eyes shone and Jordan drew in his breath at the sight of her, suddenly radiant with happiness. Light seemed to stream from her, cruelly illuminating his own life where there was satisfaction and brief pleasure, but little joy.

He pulled open the door. "Perhaps you'll leave now," he said coldly. "My schedule has been disrupted enough for one morning."

Chapter Four

Jordan stood at his hotel window, looking out as the lights of Paris came on in the twilight. From his suite high up on the Champs Elysées he had a good view of the city, but he was blind to its beauty. His mind was on the next day's meeting with a man whose backing he was determined to win for an international project.

He made a sound of annoyance as the phone rang, and he strode across the room to answer it. "Yes?"

Lorrayne's husky chuckle reached him down the line. "Surprise, surprise."

He controlled his annoyance at having his concentration disturbed. "It certainly is. I was just about to call you," he added untruthfully. "I wanted to apologize for canceling our date. I had to dash off suddenly."

"Darling, I forgive you. Aren't I always very forgiving?"

"The soul of generosity," he said mechanically. Politeness forced him to ask, "How is it in England? Wet and windy, I expect."

"Perhaps, darling. But I'm not in England. I'm somewhere *much* nearer."

"Just how much?" he asked with misgiving.

"I'm in Paris. To be exact I'm right down the hall."

"What are you doing here?"

"Darling, that's not very welcoming. I'm on my way to Venice for a few days, and I just stopped over. Surely you're going to join me for a drink?"

"Of course," he said reluctantly.

"I'm in room fifty-four."

He hung up and passed his hand across his eyes in the weary gesture that was now habitual. On the other hand, he needed a drink, and dining with Lorrayne might be preferable to dining alone. He found it all too easy to start brooding.

He no longer hated Veronica for deceiving him. It was natural that her daughter's life came before truth and fair play. But he was troubled by another feeling that went back to his days in the institution, and to Jeff, his one close friend. They'd raided orchards, shared homework and given each other alibis.

But then Jeff's parents had come and taken him away to a world from which Jordan was shut out. It was the last time in his life that he'd cried.

Veronica's glowing happiness as she thought of the future that she and Holly would share had given him the same sensation of pressing his nose against a windowpane, and for a moment he'd been possessed by the same dumb misery.

Luckily his business studies had included a course of elementary psychology, so he was well equipped to deal with an overreaction that really had nothing to do with Veronica at all. But his thoughts were troublesome companions, and he was glad of Lorrayne's company.

A few minutes later he was knocking on the door of her suite. She opened it and stood smiling at him. She was a poised beauty in her thirties with chestnut hair and green eyes. She'd dressed skillfully in the autumn tints that were becoming to her, and her jewelry was solid gold. "My poor darling," she said, ushering him in. "How tired you look!"

"No more than usual," he said, doing little to disguise his irritation, which she'd noticed.

Lorrayne drew him into the room and closed the door. "Well, I know you've been extra busy because I've seen almost nothing of you for weeks," she said, slipping her arms around his neck. "In fact, I've been very neglected."

"Is that why you're here?" he asked wryly.

She stopped with her lips an inch from his and laughed. "I told you, I'm on my way to my little Venetian villa." She pulled away without kissing him and went to the liquor cabinet. "It's pure chance we're in Paris on the same night," she said gaily, "although I admit I chose this hotel because this is where you always stay." There was a knock at the door. "Get that, will you, darling?" she called, vanishing into the bedroom.

A waiter with a table on wheels was outside the door. The table was laid for two, and the meal was steak, done as he preferred, and accompanied by a crisp green salad and a bottle of his favorite wine.

"I ordered dinner for us," Lorrayne said, appearing when the waiter had gone. "I thought it would be cozier here."

"And we could hardly have gone out with you dressed like that," Jordan agreed, eyeing the black chiffon peignoir she'd changed into. Beneath it was another garment of the same material that might have been a negligee, but didn't look designed for sleeping.

As they ate she gossiped amusingly about their mutual acquaintances. He laughed but found it an effort. It had never troubled him before that her wit relied on cruelty, but tonight it annoyed him. Over coffee he said, "I didn't know you were planning a trip to the villa."

She shrugged. "I just suddenly felt like it. You ought to come, too. It would do you good to get away for a few days."

He replied noncommittally and took his liqueur over to the sofa. Lorrayne followed him and sat down. She'd allowed the peignoir to slip down from her shoulders, exposing the plunging neckline of the flimsy gown beneath and the swell of her magnificent breasts.

He smiled politely, wondering why black lingerie was supposed to give a woman mystery. Real mystery was when you desired someone to madness as she sat there huddled up in an old duffle coat whose bulk hid her shape. And when you took her in your arms, seeking the lines of her sweet body through the confining clothes, and tasting the honey on her lips, *that* was mystery—and delight and torment and wonder. That was joy and anguish, hope and despair, terrible frustration and miraculous fulfillment.

"Darling, I don't think you heard a word I said." Lorrayne's husky murmur was tinged with reproach.

"I'm sorry," he said hastily.

"Never mind." Lorrayne leaned close to him. "We don't need to talk," she said softly, and laid her mouth on his.

Mechanically he put his arms around her, struggling to respond. But the muskiness of her perfume struck his senses unpleasantly, making him long for the scent of spring and wildflowers. She was pressed against him, but he felt no answering thrill. His mind was filled with images of a naked body, half turned in demure provocation, enticing while it concealed: Veronica as he'd wanted her so long ago, as he'd wanted her the night they'd met again—as he wanted her now.

After a long moment Lorrayne moved back to regard him questioningly, and he forced a smile. "I guess you were right. I'm a lot more tired than I thought I was," he said hastily.

"Well, I know how to put that right."

"No." He stopped her moving close again. "I need a good night's sleep."

"What you need is a few days in Venice, really relaxing, darling."

"You go on tomorrow, and I'll call you when I'm free." He kissed her briefly and rose, heading for the door. "Good night Lorrayne," he said hurriedly. "Thank you for a delightful evening."

He exited before she could say anything more. Lorrayne sat still, watching the closed door, her hard eyes narrowing thoughtfully.

A NIGHT OF PASSION

* * *

Jordan's negotiations with the Paris banker went badly, by his standards. He got the backing he wanted, but at a price he hadn't meant to pay. For the first time in all his years of traveling, his mind was on someone he'd left behind. He called the surgeon to ask about Holly's checkup and was told it had gone well, but his restlessness continued.

On the morning of the actual operation he took a taxi to Paris's Orly airport. Once there he planned to call Lorrayne to say he would be in Venice that afternoon. A few days with her should restore their relationship to its old comfortable footing and enable both of them to forget the aberration of the other night.

He looked at his watch. Eleven o'clock. Holly would be having her premedication about now. Veronica would be sitting beside her.

There was a wait for the next Venice plane, and he decided to have a snack before he put through the call. Absently he noticed that the flight for London would be leaving shortly.

As he ate he checked the time again. There was still no hurry. Veronica was probably squeezing Holly's hand and giving her a quick final kiss, and the little girl would smile back sleepily. Then they would wheel her away and Veronica would watch her until the last moment.

"Flight 522 to London is ready for boarding through Gate 35."

It was time he bought a ticket and called Lorrayne. He rose, went to the airline desk and gave his destination. The woman handed over his ticket and he glanced at it briefly. Then his brow furrowed in annoyance. "This is incorrect," he said. "I asked for a ticket to Venice."

"Pardon, monsieur, the destination you gave me was London."

"That's impossible."

"Monsieur, you said you wanted a ticket to London. But if there has been a mistake I can issue a new ticket."

She reached out her hand. Jordan stepped back sharply. "No," he said. "There's been no mistake."

He seized his bag and put it onto the belt at the check-in desk. In another moment he had his boarding pass and was running in the direction of the departure gate for the flight to London.

It was strange, Veronica thought, to long for something and then be so terrified when it came. Holly was on the operating table now, her life in the hands of strangers.

She thought of all the things that could go wrong and had to fight down her dread. The surgeon had assured her that the operation was routinely successful, but she couldn't rid herself of the picture of Holly, lying still, her eyes closed, having to travel into the darkness before she could be brought back to normal life. She was so small to make such a dangerous journey alone.

Veronica had been allowed into Holly's cheerful little ward while she was given her premedication. She'd longed to take her child into her arms for one last hug before the first drug was administered, but she controlled her emotion so that Holly wouldn't suspect how frightened she was. Instead she'd smiled and tweaked the end of Holly's nose.

The anesthesiologist had come in. He was a surprisingly young man wearing huge spectacles who gave the little girl a broad grin. "You're not worried, are you?" he inquired gently.

"Bit," she said, her eyes on the needle.

"Don't be. One little prick of this and you'll vanish and we'll have to do the operation without you."

Holly had giggled at that, and while she was still giggling he gently lifted her arm, and it was done.

Veronica, sitting on her other side, took her hand. Already sleepy, Holly turned her head slowly and whispered, "Don't worry, Mommy. It's all right—honest."

Her eyes drooped and closed. Veronica thought, *She was comforting me.*

Now she was free to take her child into her arms and hold her close for a long moment before her doctor set up the IV. At last she laid Holly gently back against the pillows, steadied herself with a deep breath, and walked slowly out of the room. A few moments later the door had opened and Holly's bed had been wheeled out into the corridor, down to the far end, and out of sight.

She'd hardly moved since then, and Holly had been gone so very long. A terrible foreboding was beginning to form inside her.

At long last there was a noise from the far end of the hall and she looked up quickly. The surgeon padded down the corridor, and quickly informed her that Holly had come through with flying colors. Shortly afterward several nurses appeared with a bed on wheels. Veronica rose to her feet and intently scrutinized Holly's pale face on the pillow.

Seeing Veronica, the nurses stopped. "She's fine, but it's normal procedure for the patient to spend the night in a recovery room. We're taking her there now."

"May I come in?"

"Give us a few minutes to get her settled, and then I'll call you." The procession passed on and Veronica sank back onto her seat.

At Heathrow airport Jordan didn't wait for his bags to appear on the conveyor belt, but went straight through Customs with only his hand luggage. He would send someone for the rest another time. What mattered was getting to the hospital as fast as possible. Once outside he shamelessly went to the head of a long lineup and hijacked the first taxi. "The Jameson Clinic," he said curtly.

As the car covered the miles he checked his watch again. He should arrive just as Holly left the operating room. With luck he would reach the waiting room while Veronica was still there. He thought of her face as he'd seen it in the past, lit up at some happy chance word or action. He wondered if her eyes would shine at the sight of him now.

They'd reached the clinic. Jordan jumped out, tossed the driver a large bill and hurried inside. "Where's Holly Grant?" he asked the receptionist.

"On the third floor, but you can't—"

Jordan had already gone.

Veronica was counting the minutes. It was half an hour since Holly had left the operating room. Surely they couldn't be much longer. "Please," she prayed, "let me be with her when she awakes."

A man's shadow loomed over her and she looked up quickly, her face brightening as she saw who it was. "Derek," she said gladly.

"I had a difficult client who wanted to talk forever," he said, sitting beside her. "But in the end I cut him short to get here."

"That was nice of you."

"Sorry I'm a bit late, but better late than never, eh? Is there any news?"

"The operation was successful. We'll be able to see her in a minute."

He slipped an arm around her shoulders. Veronica leaned against him, feeling drained. It would have been good to have had him here earlier, as he'd half promised, but his solid presence was welcome now.

Neither of them heard the door open at the end of the hall. Nor did they see Jordan come through and stand motionless at the sight of them.

"Tired?" Derek asked.

"Mmm."

"You've had a rough time, but I'm here now." He kissed her forehead. "Hey, come on, there's nothing to cry about."

"I'm not crying," she said indignantly, fumbling for a handkerchief. "It's just that she looked so tiny."

He tightened his arm into a robust hug and spoke in a rallying tone, both of which jarred on her slightly. "She's going to be all right. Give her a few weeks and she'll be running around kicking a football and getting into mischief. The three of us will have wonderful times."

She wished he would just hold her quietly. Her frayed nerves couldn't cope with heartiness just now. But he meant well, so she smiled and squeezed his hand.

The door to the recovery room opened, and a nurse appeared, smiling. "You can go in now," she said.

Veronica exchanged an eager look with Derek, and they rose to go in quickly. The nurse closed the door behind them and turned to speak to the man she thought she'd glimpsed at the end of the hall. But there was no one in sight.

Veronica had expected Holly's hospital stay to be a long one after such major surgery, but the doctor told her Holly might be home in ten days. "She's healed very fast, and now that the oxygen is being pumped around efficiently she's full of energy," he said.

Her heart overflowed with thanks. She would have liked to tell Jordan what he'd done for her, but she never heard from him, although the surgeon said he'd called the hospital.

She was trying to compose a letter to him one evening, when her phone rang and she heard Jordan's voice for the first time since she'd stormed into his office. "They tell me Holly's going home tomorrow," he said without preamble.

"Yes. It's wonderful to see her so well again—"

Jordan cut her off, not rudely but like a man trying to get through a crowded schedule. "I'm glad to hear that. I've been thinking about her convalescence. She should have a few weeks in a good place in the country before she finally goes home."

"I'm not asking you to pay for a convalescent home as well—"

"I didn't mean that. I have a country house where I'd like Holly to stay. If she's getting active again she'll need some room to play, and your apartment doesn't have a garden."

"That's true, but Jordan, I..." She stopped, embarrassed by her thoughts.

"It's all right, you needn't worry that I'll bother you. I won't be there. It's close enough to London for her to get back easily for checkups, but quiet enough for her to finish recovering. Do I have your agreement?"

"Of course, I think it's a wonderful idea. Jordan, please let me th—"

"Good, then I'll pass you over to Kate who's handling the arrangements." His voice became more distant as if he'd turned away, and Veronica just heard him say, "Take care of this for me, please, Kate."

Jordan's secretary came on the line and explained that a car would call for her the next morning, take her to the clinic to collect Holly, and drive them to their destination in the country. Veronica had to pinch herself to make sure she wasn't dreaming.

She felt a moment's sadness for Jordan, who'd brought her a happiness he couldn't share. He'd been almost curt, seeming to tick off items as he spoke in a businesslike fashion. He was a conscientious man, performing his side of their bargain to the full. But it was Derek who'd taken the trouble to come and be with her at the hospital, she reminded herself.

She stared when she saw the elegant limousine that drew up at the door the next day. It swept her to the clinic in more luxury than she'd ever known, and soon she was in Holly's room. Her daughter was already dressed, her cheeks rosy and glowing, and anxious to be off to start her new life.

But first she scampered around to say goodbye to the nurses who'd cared for her, as well as an orderly to whom she apologized for some mischief that, with her mother's eyes on her, she left carefully vague. The young man winked and assured her that all was forgiven. "Come along," Veronica said, taking her hand, "before I hear things that are better not told."

On the journey Veronica explained that they were going to Elmbridge, a country house that belonged to "a friend." Holly, who loved the country, could hardly contain her excitement. She glued herself to the window and grew more and more delighted as London fell away and they could see greenery.

At last they were driving between tall hedges, and then there was a wrought iron gate leading to a long drive, with a red brick house at the end. As they neared a door opened and a middle-aged woman came onto the front step.

"I'm Mrs. Hendricks," she said as they got out. "I'll be looking after you. The house is all ready."

Veronica was curious about the kind of home Jordan had chosen for himself when he wanted to get away from the bustle of wheeling and dealing. She was rather surprised that he ever wanted to get away from it at all, and her surprise grew as they followed the housekeeper. Outside the house looked large, but inside it was cozy and warm. The hall had polished parquet flooring with rag rugs. The staircase was broken halfway up by a small landing, lit by leaded windows, through which Holly stared, entranced, at the huge gardens. "Mommy, look!" she breathed.

Her room was a little girl's dream, with big windows looking out onto the gardens, and cheerful decorations. Veronica found her room next door. She loved the four-poster bed in polished oak with the flowered curtains, which with the biscuit-colored carpet, white walls and nineteenth-century fashion prints created a restful atmosphere.

They went to explore outside and found part of the gardens formal and carefully tended and part a kind of wilderness with a small wood and a stream. Here they discovered the elms and the bridge that had given the house its name. With difficulty Veronica dissuaded Holly from taking off her shoes and paddling. It was hard to be firm because she, too, had a sudden urge to get her feet wet. In this idyllic place, free from care for the first time in months, she felt like a child let out of school.

Holly's room looked even more welcoming when Veronica had unpacked the books and toys she'd brought. She managed to persuade her daughter to lie down for an afternoon nap, but Holly was too excited to sleep, and when Veronica looked in she saw Holly on the window seat, staring blissfully out at her surroundings.

Mrs. Hendricks showed her over the rest of the house, which was as pleasant and comfortably lived in as the rooms she'd already seen. "You must tell me which rooms not to go in," she said.

"There are no rooms you can't go in," Mrs. Hendricks told her, surprised.

"I mean Mr. Cavendish's rooms." She saw the older woman frowning and asked, "Isn't this Jordan Cavendish's house?"

"I don't know any Mr. Cavendish. The only person I saw was Mrs. Adams when she came to look the place over. But now that I think of it, she said she worked for a Mr. Cavendish."

"But I don't understand. You say Mrs. Adams came to look the house over? When?"

"A few days ago. She said her boss was looking for something like this to rent."

Veronica bit back her exclamation of astonishment. Jordan had spoken as though he owned the house. Now it seemed he'd taken it purposely for Holly, but he didn't want Veronica to know.

That night she kept the connecting door open between her room and Holly's. Once she crept in and sat by the window in the darkness, pervaded by a deep contentment as she listened to the strong, steady sound of her daughter's breathing.

She'd been shaken by what she'd learned today. Why should any man want to conceal such an act of kindness?

But you know why, said a voice in her mind. Because he's afraid you'll think he's beginning to accept Holly as his own, and he'll never do that.

It hadn't been kindness that had made Jordan take this house but a determination to keep his word to the last penny. Paradoxically, his seeming generosity was an act of rejection.

She remembered how he'd stood at the window in his office, with his back to her, and the sudden set of his shoulders as he resolved how to act. Until then she'd half believed that he really couldn't remember their lovemaking. But there was something about the decisiveness of that movement that convinced her he knew the truth and had deliberately chosen to deny it.

Veronica crept to the bed where her child was sleeping, possessed by a surge of fierce protectiveness for the little girl. Holly looked as gentle and vulnerable as Jordan had looked the night she'd held him in her arms and conceived his daughter.

And suddenly she remembered the night of their reunion. *"You were the only magic I ever knew."* She felt his lips trembling with longing against hers, and closed her eyes, seared with pity for him. She'd done only what she had to do, but it was terrible nonetheless. He lived in a world where trust barely existed. He'd called Veronica the only person he'd ever really trusted. And now he would never trust her again.

She bent and gently kissed Holly before slipping out of the room.

Chapter Five

Once Holly's health was restored, her mischievous disposition became more marked. "That's the last time I ever suggest hide and seek," Veronica said breathlessly one morning, coming into the kitchen and flopping down on a chair. "The little monkey knows all the hiding places in this garden."

Mrs. Hendricks placed a cup of tea in front of her, and Veronica drank it thankfully.

"Come on, Mommy," Holly begged from the garden door.

"Later, darling. Give the old lady time to rest."

Holly giggled. "You're not an old lady."

"I wasn't before that game; I am now. One more will put me in my dotage."

They'd settled easily into the pleasant country life. Mrs. Hendricks was an excellent cook who'd set herself to building up her patient, and the little girl was filling out daily. To Veronica's dismay the same thing was happening to her, and she began a program of rigorous exercise to keep her model figure.

They played lively games in the morning, and in the afternoon Holly was supposed to nap. But mostly she lay on her bed and read. She had a practical turn of mind, enjoying crime, science fiction and anything that stretched her intelligence. She could juggle figures with a speed and accuracy far beyond her years, and startled her mother by borrowing advanced math books from the local library and seeming to enjoy them.

The day after they arrived, Kate had telephoned to ask if they were comfortable and told Veronica to call if there was anything she wanted. Veronica had understood that there would be no direct contact from Jordan. He'd promised not to trouble her, and Jordan Cavendish was a man of his word.

But though he didn't come to the house he troubled her in other ways. She now had long hours in idyllic surroundings with little to occupy her mind. Whenever she tried to plan the future she was haunted by dreams of another life, the one she'd briefly believed in that night by the river with Jordan. *We never really left each other—not in our hearts.*

It was true—she'd known it at once. Her heart had never given him up. The magic of that night had enchanted her, too, making her forget everything, including the way she'd contrived their meeting and the revelation she had to make to him. Her love had reawakened, filling her soul and body, inspiring her kiss with ardor.

She tried to brush aside the memory of his lips moving against hers, skillful where once they'd been unpracticed, yet with the same tender urgency that had won her love before. But her mouth seemed to have retained the imprint of his. Waking or sleeping, she always sensed Jordan was with her, tormenting her with the thought of what could never be, for she knew she could never have a future with a man who'd chosen to deny their child.

To her dismay she was taking a long time to shake off the fear that had haunted her for months. It was too soon to be entirely light-hearted, and although Holly grew stronger by the day Veronica found herself troubled by dark thoughts. She had to struggle to stop herself supervising Holly's every moment, or saying "Don't" to every new thing the child wanted to do. She controlled those instincts, determined not to spoil the little girl's happiness, but the strain was taking its toll.

Once she began to tell Derek, but he roared with laughter and said, "Come on, darling. It's over now. Let it go." She didn't try to discuss her feelings with him again, but inwardly she was lonely in a way she'd never been conscious of before.

Summer had arrived now, and some days she was able to do her exercises outdoors on the patio, which led into the rear living room through a pair of French windows. She'd just finished one afternoon when she heard a car arrive at the front. She waited for the sound of the doorbell, but it didn't come. "Mrs. Hendricks is out," she said to Holly. "I'd better go and see who it is."

Holly murmured something unintelligible without raising her head from a math book, and Veronica went through the house to the front door. She opened it to find Jordan's sleek silver car parked there, but no sign of Jordan himself.

She darted back the way she'd come, and when she reached the door to the living room she stopped.

Jordan was standing in the open French windows, his eyes fixed on Holly whose head was still bent over her book, with a look in them that made Veronica stand silent. She'd never seen anyone look so sad. At the same time there was a faint smile playing around the corners of his mouth, as though the little girl's fierce concentration gave him a curious delight.

Holly heaved an exasperated sigh and said, "Oh, rats' knickers!"

Veronica gave a smothered choke of laughter. Jordan looked up and saw her and for a moment their eyes met in pure amusement. He laughed aloud and for the first time Holly realized he was there. "Good morning," she said politely. "I met you once, didn't I? Are you any good at math?"

To a man whose computerlike mind kept him on top of the financial jungle this question came as a shock. But he recovered admirably and said, "Pretty good."

"Oh, lovely, you can tell me what I'm doing wrong," Holly said happily.

"Holly," Veronica protested, "that isn't a very polite way to welcome someone."

"But she's right," Jordan said. "Once you've started on a problem you should stick with it. I was just the same—" He broke off sharply.

At that same instant Veronica became aware of the leotard outlining every curve of her body. It was like a second skin, revealing by concealment, emphasizing the roundness of her hips in contrast to her tiny waist, and the slender length of her legs. She picked up a towel but found it only big enough to go around her neck.

"I came to see how you were," Jordan said.

"That's nice of you. I'll just go change," she said quickly and hurried out. When she returned she'd changed into a demure dress, but she might have spared the effort. Jordan was sitting with Holly, explaining how to tackle her problem, and although he looked up briefly, it was plain he was occupied. Veronica left without disturbing them.

"Got it now?" Jordan asked. "Or would you like me to go over it again?"

"No, thank you," Holly said. "I understood."

"Are you sure? This is a rather advanced book and you can't be much more than seven."

"I'll be nine next month," she told him, offended.

There was a strange silence before Jordan asked, "Did your mother tell you to say that?" Then, seeing Holly's bewildered look, he went on hastily. "Forget it. I didn't mean anything. It's just that...you look younger than nine."

"That's because I'm a bit small," Holly said with a sigh. "Mommy's short, and she says I may be, too, but I think now I'm well again I might grow very fast. At least, I hope so."

"Does being small matter so much?"

"I hate people thinking I'm younger than I am—it makes them treat me like a baby. When you said 'This is a rather advanced book' just now, you sounded exactly like Miss Adderway."

It was plain that this was a crime of no small order, and Jordan hastened to apologize before asking, "Who's Miss Adderway?"

"She's my schoolteacher. I've had to miss a lot of school recently, but I've worked terribly hard to keep up, especially at math, because it's fun. She keeps saying 'Now, you won't know this...' and when she finds I do she's cross. It's funny, isn't it? You'd think she'd be glad. I mean, she's a teacher."

"Yes, but she's also a person, and a pretty silly one from the sound of it," Jordan said. "Teachers don't always like a really bright pupil. I was good at math, too, and instead of being pleased, the teacher called me a show-off."

Holly beamed with pleasure at this understanding. "Once Miss Adderway asked a question and I was the only person who put a hand up. I kept it up for ages, but she pretended not to see me."

"I remember the teacher once asking me a question I couldn't answer," Jordan said, "and he sneered 'Oh, there *is* something you don't know.'"

"That's mean," Holly said severely.

Until now he'd forgotten that painful bewilderment, but for a moment it flickered again, then died at the little girl's indignant empathy. He had a strange feeling of having discovered a comrade. "That's what I felt," he agreed. "But I was a child, and what can a child do about a mean adult?"

"Nothing," Holly said wisely.

They looked at each other in mutual appreciation.

"Look, you mustn't let it get to you," Jordan added. "Remember it's only a kind of jealousy, and don't be intimidated by it."

"Was that how you managed?"

Jordan grimaced. "I had problems you don't have. I lived in an institution. It was called a 'home' but that's just what it wasn't. You have a mother who—" he hesitated "—who'd do anything in the world for you."

Holly nodded. "Mommy tries to understand, but she doesn't really know what it's like," she said, "not the way you do."

"No, I guess you have to have been through it to know. It can't really be explained."

Veronica put her head around the door to say, "I hope you'll stay and have tea with us."

"Yes, thank you." Jordan rose and followed her out into the kitchen. "I meant what I said about not troubling you," he continued, "but I was in this area and thought I'd look in to see how you were doing."

Veronica smiled. "You can see for yourself how perky Holly is. I'm glad you came, Jordan. I was afraid I might not have a chance to thank you for letting us stay here."

He colored. "I told you that you could have everything you needed. I didn't just mean the operation. The important thing is that Holly's recovering."

"I still make her get plenty of rest, but in between her naps she's full of tricks. In fact, we won't need to trouble you much longer."

"There's no hurry for you to leave," he said gruffly. "The house is yours for as long as you need it."

She'd meant to reveal that she knew the house was rented, but she couldn't find the right words. "The kettle's boiling."

She was glad that Holly was with them at tea. It saved her from having to examine what she was thinking and feeling at seeing Jordan again. She'd calmed her inner disturbance at the way he'd taken her by surprise, but she couldn't subdue the little stabs of pleasure that assailed her when he turned his handsome head to speak to Holly, or gave the little girl a smile. Holly chatted to him with complete confidence. Jordan did more listening than talking, and Veronica realized that he looked like a man whose attention had been caught despite himself.

"Mommy," Holly said, "I don't really want any more. I'm a bit sleepy."

"All right then, off to bed," Veronica said.

Holly bade Jordan good-night and made her way sleepily upstairs. Veronica came down a few minutes later to find Jordan in the living room gazing out over the grounds, with the countryside beyond fading to a soft violet as twilight fell. He looked around quickly as he heard her. "Is she all right?" he asked.

"She's fast asleep."

"Does she always get tired so suddenly?"

"No, but today she didn't get her afternoon rest."

"Because of me?"

"Only partly. She should have gone upstairs before you arrived, but I let her wriggle out of it. She usually lies there reading, and since she was reading anyway, I left her, but I won't do it again."

"She's really clever, isn't she? Not that I know much about children, but I know about figures, and what she was asking me about today would have taxed an eleven-year-old. She picked it up right away."

Veronica nodded. "She's got a tough little mind, very factual. 'Scientific' and 'logical' are her favorite words right now. She uses them to outwit me because she knows I'm neither."

"No, you were always more of a dreamer, weren't you? I can't see Holly yearning to play Juliet."

Veronica smiled. "Not unless she could rewrite the play to make Juliet analyze the potion before drinking it."

The note of regret in her voice made Jordan frown. "It's not her fault that she's different from you, Veronica."

"Good heavens, I'm not set on making her a duplicate of myself. She's her own person. It's just that if we were alike I could help her more. I overheard what she said to you about my not knowing what it's like for her, and it's true." She gave a self-deprecating laugh. "I was all right at school but no one could have called me brilliant. I have this awful feeling that I'm failing her."

Jordan shook his head firmly. "You can't call yourself a failure when you've produced such a marvelous child."

"She *is* marvelous, isn't she?" Veronica agreed at once, then checked herself for fear of becoming garrulous. But she couldn't stop her eyes from glowing with pleasure at his praise.

The next moment the glow faded as Jordan asked, "Who is her father?"

Veronica's lips tightened. She'd promised not to claim Jordan as Holly's father but there was nothing else she could say. "I don't want to discuss that."

"Is it Derek?" he persisted.

"No, I've only known Derek a few months."

"And you slept with Holly's father almost as soon as we said goodbye, didn't you?" he demanded curtly. "Or were you sleeping with him all the time you kept me at a distance?"

"I didn't keep you at a distance. You kept yourself at a distance because you didn't want to become involved."

"What about you? You didn't want involvement, either."

She was silent, remembering how she'd let him think she was as detached as he, because if he'd suspected the depth of her love he might have run in the opposite direction. He'd been like a wild animal that she could entice toward her only by not being too eager.

There'd been pain in those bittersweet days, but also a piercing joy she was sure she would never know again, and the memory brought a faint, melancholy smile to her lips. Jordan saw it and drew in his breath, cursing himself for all kinds of a fool. "He must have really been something," he said bitterly.

"If you mean Holly's father," Veronica said softly. "Yes, he was wonderful."

"Wonderful," he snapped. "Wonderful enough to make you play fast and loose while you were keeping me on a string. Did it amuse you to play games with him knowing that I was crazy about you?"

"You were never crazy about me. You were passing the time."

"Never..." Jordan gave a growl of anger as his control snapped, and he reached out to pull her into his arms. He held her trapped there while he blazed, "I thought about you night and day, and shall I tell you something that'll give you a real laugh? I put you on a pedestal. I idolized you as someone perfect and untouchable, and all the time you—" He broke off, his breath coming in ragged gasps. Veronica's flushed face was raised toward him, her body pressed against his. A tremor shook him, and with a groan he bent his head to cover her mouth with his own.

At the touch of his lips, Veronica felt a battle start within her. This was the man who'd rejected their child, forcing her to set her name to a lie, the man she must not, dare not love. But he was also the man who could make her pulse race like no other, whose touch could cause her bones to melt and her heart to flame into life. She'd deluded herself that she could see Jordan in proper perspective, but the headlong torrent of feeling that possessed her now distorted everything, making her conscious of nothing but him.

She could feel anger and frustration in Jordan's kiss as he demanded her surrender. Her heart and body would have given up to him willingly, but her mind tried to hold out against the delight that was stealing insidiously over her. She fought her response down. He could never be hers, and her pride rebelled against letting him suspect how easily she might have been his.

But he was moving his mouth against hers with terrifying skill, subtly persuading her until her lips parted, despite her inner resistance. She sighed helplessly as his tongue slid between them and sought out the dark warmth within. She could feel the change in him as she yielded. His tense muscles relaxed, making it easier to fit her body against the contours of his. His tongue flickered against the satiny skin of her mouth and a tremor went through him.

She'd longed for him so much, and now her reawakened feelings were too strong for her. Unable to stop herself, she reached up to slide one arm around his neck and twine her fingers in his hair.

The past wasn't over as she'd tried to tell herself. It would never be over as long as Jordan's kiss could bring her heart to blazing life. The young, innocent Veronica still lived in this wary, embattled woman who could fight the man she loved, but melt at the first touch of his lips.

How many times had they clasped each other like this, exchanging fevered kisses that they knew must stop short of fulfillment? She'd fought to keep her young passion behind walls of caution, and learned, too late, that caution burned up in the heat of love. That fatal discovery had started the chain of events that had brought her here today, in Jordan's arms again, while past and present mingled in a timeless kiss.

She was burningly aware of his body in intimate contact with hers. The fierce excitement that possessed him was uncompromisingly clear even through their clothes. Forbidden images chased through her head, images of the two of them together. She must make him stop while she still had some control, but on that thought her arms seemed to tighten around him of their own accord.

He began to kiss the sensitive skin just below her ear. The sensation sent pleasure through her, and a soft moan escaped her. He heard it through the thundering of his own heart, and the two seemed to trigger an explosion of warning inside his head. He jerked back abruptly, gasping as he looked at her in shock.

For a moment they stared at each other, each seeking in the other's face a mirror of his or her own bewilderment. The old passion had overtaken them again, but now it was a thousand times stronger and more dangerous.

Veronica tried to draw away, but he held her, pulling her close to kiss her again. Her lips were still burning, and she raised them willingly to his and felt the fierce desire that only he could arouse. She knew she should resist him, but she had no power to reject what she so ardently longed for. If only something would happen to save her....

"Mommy!"

The voice from upstairs was faint, but it pierced through the haze of her passion. "Mommy!" she heard Holly's voice again.

With a strength born of fear, she wrenched herself out of Jordan's arms and said desperately, "Why did you ever come here? Go away, Jordan, and leave me and my daughter alone."

She fled, and a moment later Jordan heard her running upstairs. He gave himself a minute to calm the turbulence in his blood and followed her. As he reached the landing Veronica was coming out of Holly's room. "Is she ill?" he demanded tensely.

"No, she just wants a drink."

Veronica hurried downstairs. Jordan went to the door of Holly's room. Her night-light was on and she was sitting up, rubbing sleep out of her eyes. She smiled when she saw him. "Hello."

"Hello," he said, advancing into the room. "I thought you were sound asleep."

"I woke up because I was thirsty." Holly patted the bed hopefully, and he sat down. "Have you fallen down?" she asked, concerned.

"No, why?"

"Your hair's all mussed, and it wasn't before."

He smoothed it hastily. "You have a nice room," he said to divert her from the subject.

"Yes, it's lovely, isn't it? I can see right out over the gardens into the trees."

"What do you do in the garden?"

"I like the wild bit at the end because Mommy and I can play hide and seek. But I can't do much where it's all tidy because Mr. Perks doesn't like it."

"Who's Mr. Perks?"

"He comes in to do the gardening. He has 'moods.' If I kick a football around he starts thinking about how long it took him to mow the lawn, and that brings one of his moods on."

"Oh, those sort of moods—the kind that come and go to suit his convenience?"

Holly giggled. "Yes, that kind."

"Is he an old man?"

"About the same as you."

"Not an old man," Jordan said hastily. "I know the type. Well, remember what I told you about the teacher, and don't give in to it. It's your lawn, not his. Why are you looking like that?" he asked, for Holly had put her head on one side and was regarding him with awe.

"I've never heard a grown-up talk that way about another grown-up before," she explained. "Usually they all gang up."

Jordan's lips twitched. "Being grown-up is a bit of a closed shop," he said. "And we like to keep it that way because a closed shop has its privileges. As you get older you'll find grown-ups will fight harder and harder to keep you out until they reckon you're old enough to think like them. That's known as 'being mature.'"

"Most grown-ups talk to children as though they were invisible," Holly pointed out. "But you're not like that."

He nodded, remembering the frustrations of his childhood. "They seem to address some point just beyond your left ear," he agreed.

"Not Mommy," Holly said quickly. "She's not like other grown-ups, either, but even she..." She trailed off and looked at him in hopeful expectation of empathy.

"But even she can't quite follow what's going on in your mind," he finished, and she smiled her relief. He took her hand, which was lying on the coverlet. "But then, we're all so different that nobody ever knows exactly what another person's feeling," he said quietly. "Sometimes you think you do. You believe you can see right into their heart and soul, and what you find there is beautiful. But that's when you should be most on your guard—" He stopped, aghast at what he was saying.

The silence lengthened while he floundered around in his mind, frantically seeking a neutral subject. Then he felt a soft pressure on his hand and realized that Holly was squeezing it comfortingly. He met her eyes and found in them the same look of fellowship that he'd seen that afternoon.

It was something he'd never known before in his life. He'd had lovers and could call a couple of men good friends, but the instinctive fellow feeling of people who are basically alike had come to him for the first time in this little girl. Shaken, he stared at her.

Veronica appeared in the doorway with Holly's drink. She stopped as she saw their hands clasped, and looked from the man to the child. What happened next astounded her. Jordan glanced at her, then back to Holly and shook his head very slightly. It was so faint as to be almost imperceptible, but to Veronica it was as though warning bells had clamored noisily. Jordan had signaled to her daughter that whatever they'd talked about must remain private between them. And Holly had given him the briefest possible nod in return.

"Here's your drink, darling," she said, advancing to the bed. "Don't keep Mr. Cavendish talking all night. He has to drive back to London."

"Yes, that's a pity," Jordan said thoughtfully. "If I'd been staying here we could have talked some more tomorrow."

"But can't you stay?" Holly asked anxiously.

"Darling, you mustn't bother Mr. Cavendish. He has a lot of work to do in London," Veronica said firmly.

Jordan shrugged. "Nothing that can't wait. But naturally if you're anxious for me to go—"

"Of course we're not," Holly broke in indignantly. "He can stay, can't he Mommy?"

Cornered, Veronica had no choice but to smile and say, "Certainly he can stay if he wants to. Go to sleep now, darling."

She kissed Holly and stood back, indicating for Jordan to leave the room ahead of her. He looked down at Holly for a moment, then bent and kissed her cheek. He left the room without looking at Veronica.

Outside she said, "I'd like to talk to you downstairs." He went down and she followed him. Once in the living room, she closed the door and said angrily, "What are you up to?"

"What do you mean?"

"You know exactly what I mean. You maneuvered Holly into inviting you so that I'd have no choice but to agree. Of all the devious, manipulative, disgraceful things to do—"

"Why is it disgraceful?" he interrupted.

"Because those tactics belong in the board room. I don't want them used on my daughter."

"*My* daughter—according to you," he said, his eyes ablaze.

"But not according to you. We signed a paper that destroyed her rights to you and yours to her. That's the end of it."

Jordan opened his mouth to speak, but stopped as if someone had struck him. He'd been about to make some threatening remark and was shocked when he realized the direction his mind was traveling. "Are you saying now that she isn't mine?" he demanded, very pale.

She faced him and said coldly, "I've already said she isn't. I said it in a legal document, duly witnessed. All you have to do is read it."

"And if I want to take an interest in Holly, you're going to prevent me, is that it?"

"I have no faith in your so-called interest. It'll last just as long as it amuses you, then you'll retreat behind that document, without a care if you break her heart."

"Is that what you really think—that I'd hurt that little girl, knowing how vulnerable she is?"

She drew a swift breath. "What would you know about her being vulnerable?"

"I know a good deal about her. She's different from other children and she needs careful handling—"

"Meaning that I'm mishandling her?" Veronica demanded furiously.

"Meaning that you're not the only person who understands her. A child needs two par—two adults. Whoever her father is, Veronica, you should have let her know him."

"Much good that would have done her," she flung at him. "Her father was a cold-blooded opportunist who never let people and their feelings get in his way."

"You painted a very different picture earlier. Which one am I supposed to be?" When she didn't answer, his face darkened. "Who was he, Veronica? *Tell me.*"

He'd moved very close to her and stood looking down. She wanted to retreat a step but found she couldn't move. She met his eyes defiantly, hoping he wouldn't notice the swift rise and fall of her breast. Jordan's breath was coming raggedly and his lips were slightly parted.

"Hello, I'm back!"

The prosaic sound of Mrs. Hendricks calling from the front hall broke the spell. Life flowed back into Veronica's limbs and she swiftly broke away. "That's the housekeeper," she said, trying to sound normal. "I'll help her make up your room. It's a pity you can't stay more than one night—"

"Can't I?"

"*No.* Tomorrow you have urgent business that makes it essential for you to go back to town."

There was a glint in his eyes that made her uncomfortable. "Is it Holly you're protecting Veronica... or yourself?"

"I'll call you when your room's ready," she said, and walked out.

Chapter Six

Holly's head appeared around the door. "Mommy said I mustn't disturb you," she hinted hopefully.

"You're not disturbing me," Jordan said at once, holding out a welcoming hand.

It was the next morning. Jordan had risen early and started work before anyone else was up. He'd installed himself in the house's old-fashioned study, and when Mrs. Hendricks took him coffee she found him on the phone to Australia. Back in the kitchen she told Veronica he'd said he was too busy to join them for breakfast.

Watching her daughter's face fall Veronica had been angry with Jordan. This was what she'd been afraid of when she'd tried to keep him away from Holly the night before. But it was better, she decided, for him to show himself in his true colors now, so that Holly could learn not to rely on his interest early on.

But she hadn't reckoned on Holly's determination, and as soon as breakfast was over the little girl crept away to the study.

Now she came into the room, her eyes bright with interest at the sight of the machine on the table before him. "It's a portable computer," he told her. "I carry it with me so that I can work wherever I am."

"What kind of work do you do?"

"I own a company that owns other companies. I buy and sell and put things together. Look—" he brought a set of graphics up onto the screen "—I've just bought a printing company to print a magazine I own. But these columns show the printers aren't working at full strength, so I'll probably buy a local newspaper to keep all the machines in use."

Holly nodded. "But why did you have to buy the printers?" she asked. "Couldn't you just have paid them to work for you?"

"I tried that but it didn't work because they weren't very efficient, and I couldn't make the boss take any notice of my complaints. But now *I'm* the boss, so I can insist on their being efficient."

"Do you have lots and lots of companies?"

"Lots and lots," he agreed, and produced a list on the screen. "And this," he added, tapping keys, "is a set of graphs showing which are making money and which aren't. The ones in red are giving me headaches."

"Because they're 'in the red'?" Holly punned gleefully.

He laughed. "That's right. But we could show them blue if we wanted." He tapped a key and the colors changed. "Now you do it."

He lifted her onto his lap and she went to work eagerly. When she'd exhausted the possibilities of color changing she begged to be shown something else, and Jordan obliged, noting with pleasure that she never needed anything explained twice. Practical things seemed to come naturally to her, and she could follow a complex set of commands as if they'd touched off a trigger in her own brain. He looked down at her, absorbed and completely happy, and felt a strange stirring in his heart.

"What do you want to do when you grow up?" he asked.

"I'm going to be an inventor and make things that will change the world," she said confidently.

"I believe you," he murmured.

"Would you like to see my latest invention? It's a special kind of eggbeater."

"I'd love to," he said truthfully.

She was off and back in a moment, clutching pieces of paper. "It's only plans just now," she confided and put them into his hand. After he'd studied them for a moment she asked anxiously, "Can you see what I mean?"

"Yes, it's very clever," he agreed.

Her idea was impractical but remarkably ingenious for a child, and the shapes and relative sizes had been worked out with great attention to detail. Holly had a gift for visualizing her concepts, and transferring them to paper. Jordan realized that her mind was already a finely honed precision instrument, and it could handle complexity. His interest began to grow.

From somewhere behind them came the sound of a man's voice. Holly looked up, alert. Her face broke into a smile and she scrambled down just as the door opened. "Derek!" she said happily.

Jordan recognized the man in the doorway as the one he'd encountered in Veronica's apartment. A tightening of the lips was his only sign of displeasure as he stood. Holly was bouncing around in excitement. She obviously regarded the intruder as an old friend, and his entrance was enough to distract her from her new friend. Jordan recalled Veronica's words about the intruder—Derek's a kind man and Holly's fond of him—and felt something startlingly like jealousy.

"Good morning," Derek said coolly at last. "Veronica told me you were here."

"Mr. Cavendish has been showing me his computer," Holly said, taking Derek's hand and pulling him eagerly to the table. "I can work it."

"Well, that's nice," Derek replied automatically.

"Look, I can make things happen." She tapped a few keys to make the colors change, and looked up into Derek's face for his approval.

"Very good," he said, smiling, "but you should get down now. Mr. Cavendish doesn't want little girls banging on his machine and possibly breaking it."

"Holly's too clever to break it," Jordan said, seeing Holly's shadowed face, and moving smoothly to seize his advantage. "She's been showing me her invention, and I was about to suggest that we put the diagrams on the screen. Would you like that?" he appealed shamelessly to Holly. At her enthusiastic response he began work.

It took only a few minutes to create the graphics, and he was rewarded by Holly's beaming face. "What's that?" Derek asked.

"It's a new kind of eggbeater," Holly told him. "I invented it."

He chuckled. "But what for? There are dozens already." He pulled her hair teasingly. "Don't be bothering yourself about that stuff, kiddie. You should be enjoying yourself."

Jordan's eyes met Holly's. He winked and she compressed her lips to stifle a giggle. "Why don't you go and tell your mother how clever you've been?" he asked.

Holly's glare told him she wasn't fooled. "You're getting rid of me so that you can talk without me," she accused.

Jordan grinned. "Of course I am. Go on."

Derek was frowning as he watched Holly skip from the room. "I'm not sure it was very tactful of you to admit that."

"You'd have denied it, I suppose?"

"Of course I would."

"And earned her scorn for insulting her intelligence."

"Look, just what are you doing here?" Derek demanded.

"'Taking my responsibilities seriously.' I believe that was what you said you wanted me to do."

"You could do that without descending unannounced and upsetting Veronica. Still, I understand you're leaving soon."

"I am now," Jordan said, eyeing him with dislike. "The less you and I see of each other the better it'll be for all concerned."

"I agree, and I don't want you putting ideas into Holly's head. She's got a pack of crazy notions as it is. It comes from spending too much time alone. It'll be good for her to get back to school and start being like other kids."

With difficulty Jordan stopped himself from shouting. "The point," he said, with careful restraint, "is that she *isn't* like other kids. She's exceptionally bright, and forcing her into a mold of mediocrity will only make her suffer."

"Nonsense! It's a phase, and she'll get over it much quicker if she isn't encouraged."

Jordan regarded him through narrowed eyes. "Has Veronica told you who Holly's father is?"

Derek gave a sudden knowing grin. "I know who he isn't," he said. "There's a document—" He stopped, his smile fading at the sight of Jordan's murderous expression.

"You're a very brave man to speak of that to me," Jordan said coldly, "but let me warn you, I tolerate no interference in my affairs."

"But this is hardly your affair," Derek said, recovering some of his courage. "You're a bit of a Johnny-come-lately in this business, aren't you? I'd like to know what right *you* have to interfere?"

Being unable to answer the question adequately soured Jordan's temper further. He began gathering his things quickly, knowing that if he stayed any longer he might do something that could land him in jail. He stormed off in search of Veronica and found her exercising.

She deliberately hadn't put on the revealing leotard but wore sweatpants and a loose shirt. She was lying on her back on the living room floor raising her legs very slowly in time to music, her eyes closed, her breasts rising and falling as she breathed deeply. The music covered the sound of Jordan's entrance and he stood undecided for a moment, waiting for her to see him. From this angle he could appreciate how incredibly tiny her waist was against the voluptuous swell of her hips as they moved rhythmically, and he gritted his teeth, refusing to be distracted.

"Poof!" she said at last, holding her stomach where the muscles were protesting. Jordan switched off the cassette player and she opened her eyes. "What are you doing here?" she demanded, obviously displeased.

"I came to talk to you. I want to know if you're really mad enough to marry that man?"

Her eyes shooting sparks, Veronica got up and sat on one arm of the sofa, gasping slightly. "Are you talking about Derek?"

"Yes. You said he wanted to marry you. What are you planning to do?"

"Well, the first thing I'm planning to do," she said indignantly, "is to refuse to be interrogated. You have no right to ask me questions. Who I marry concerns me, and *only* me."

"There you're wrong. It concerns Holly, as well. How you could have considered giving her a stepfather with all the subtle, razor-sharp perception of a donkey is something that baffles me."

"You've got nerve criticizing Derek," she said hotly.

Jordan groaned. "Spare me the speech about how kind he is. There's a certain sort of kindness—allied to stupidity—that's the next thing to cruelty. If you inflict him on Holly you'll be doing something cruel—despite all your good intentions."

"Meaning I'm stupid?"

"Meaning *he's* stupid!"

"Stupid by your standards, perhaps. Stupid because he doesn't spend his life making money, because other things are important to him. He's been there when I needed someone to hold on to. He left work to come and be with me in the hospital when Holly had her operation." She saw his mouth twist wryly. "Yes, go on, sneer."

"Was I sneering?"

"What else? It's hilarious to you, isn't it? The idea that someone could take time off from money-making to show their feelings must strike you as the biggest laugh of all time."

"It does now," he agreed quietly.

"I'll bet it does. Derek gave me his time and that means everything to me."

"If he's so wonderful why didn't he raise the money himself rather than let you come to me? Did he ever object to you posing naked?"

"He understood about that because he loves me—"

"Give me patience!" he broke in furiously. "If you think that, you don't know the first thing about love. A man who loved you would have been torn apart by those pictures. He'd have sold his house, gone in rags, mortgaged his very soul, *anything* to keep other men from seeing what belonged to him. And now you're seriously planning to let him become Holly's father when he doesn't know the first thing about her?"

"And you do, I suppose?"

"Yes, I do. I know what it's like for her because I went through it myself. I had damn fool teachers who called me a disruptive influence. Sure, I was disruptive! I was bored to tears with what they were teaching because I'd gone way beyond it. I nearly became delinquent because I was so bored, and if you think

I'm going to stand aside and watch while the same thing happens to Holly—''

"You're not going to have any say in Holly's future."

"Would you like to bet on that?" he demanded.

"I don't need to bet. I've got a piece of paper with your signature on it that says I'd win in any court in the country."

"If you throw that in my face again I'll... And while we're on the subject, who gave you the right to show it to him? I thought we were going to keep it between the two of us?"

"I didn't show it to him, but I had to tell him about it to explain why you were paying for the operation."

"Otherwise he might have entertained some unworthy suspicions about what I was getting in return, eh?" Jordan demanded with grim hilarity. "Well, it's nice to know the saintly Derek has some human failings, after all."

"That was a thoroughly vulgar thing to say," she snapped.

He knew it, and was furious with himself for losing control of his temper. "I'm sorry," he said curtly. "But I want to know what you're going to do about Derek."

"I suppose that's how you talk to your employees?" she observed sarcastically. "'Smith, I want to know what you're going to do about the crisis. Brown, I want to know what you're going to do about timekeeping.' You have the right to demand answers from them, Jordan, but not from me."

He ran his fingers wearily through his hair. "Very well, will you *please* tell me what you intend to do about Derek?"

"No, I won't. I'm not answerable to you for what I do or how I raise my daughter. And I'd like you to leave this house right now, before Holly discovers that we're fighting. It would upset her."

Jordan set his chin pugnaciously at her order, but before he could say anything a noise from outside caught his attention. He looked into the garden to see Holly kicking a football around with Derek and squealing with laughter.

He looked at Veronica for a moment. Then he walked out without a word, and a few minutes later she heard the sound of his car disappearing down the driveway.

It was a happy, relaxed day, spent doing nothing in particular, the sort of day Veronica had once thought she and Holly would never know again. It was perverse of her, therefore, to feel on edge, as though something was indefinably wrong. Derek was the same as always—bluff, genial, predictable—attributes that had once been so reassuring. Even his occasional lapses into pomposity hadn't troubled her too much, although now she was more edgily aware of them. Either that or they were happening more often.

When Holly had been sent up for her nap, Derek drew Veronica into the garden for a stroll. She tried to relax, knowing he loved her with a good, solid affection that wouldn't change. It was she who'd changed, she admitted reluctantly. She was fond of Derek, but she could no longer fool herself that what she felt was love.

Love was the feeling of the air crackling with electricity because one man had appeared. It was the sense of danger he could impart merely by being there, and the bittersweet magic that flooded her at the thought of him. Love was the realization that there was only one man in the world for you, the torment of knowing he could never be yours, but that no one else would do.

"This is a nice place, all right," Derek was saying. "But you'll be glad to get away."

It wasn't a question, she noticed, but a statement. She had an impulse to say she wouldn't be glad at all, but suppressed it as tactless. "I'll be glad when Holly is completely recovered," she said. "But she needs a little more time."

"But you don't want to wait until the last minute. It's a very uncomfortable position for you, with him free to wander in and out. What's more, I don't like your being under an obligation to him."

"I'll always be that, whether we're here or not."

"Nonsense, it was no more than his duty. Besides, he's rolling in wealth. You don't owe him anything, and don't let him fool you that you do."

"Derek, he hasn't asked for anything except that paper."

"Well, I'm very glad you've got his denial in writing. Once we're married Holly will be my daughter, and I don't want him getting any funny ideas."

"What kind of funny ideas?" she demanded, staring at him.

"You should have heard the way he was talking to me about her. He's getting possessive and I don't like it." Derek laughed complacently. "But I told him he could put a stop to that."

"*You* told Jordan...?" she asked, wondering if she'd heard right.

"Certainly I did. I made it plain to him he had no business interfering after all these years. He deserted you when you needed him."

Veronica's eyes widened. "You actually said that to him?"

"Not precisely in those words, but he got the point. He became very disconcerted and left the room quickly. I could tell he was ashamed."

Veronica had a wild desire to laugh as she pictured the scene. Remembering Jordan's murderous mood when he'd found her, she knew what had made him walk out on Derek, and it wasn't shame. "He didn't exactly desert me," she said uneasily. "In a sense, I deserted him."

Derek laughed so heartily that it grated on her. "Come on, darling, that's just romanticizing. Don't start rewriting the past so that Jordan Cavendish looks like a victim. You've told me yourself how he browbeat you into feeling you mustn't ever make any claims on him—"

"I never said he browbeat me," she protested.

He shrugged. "Well, the exact word isn't important."

"I should have thought that as a lawyer you'd know the exact word can be very important."

"All right, all right," he said placatingly. "However you like to put it. But you can't deny that you'd have told him about the baby if he hadn't made you feel he wouldn't want to know. I remember you telling me that."

"Yes, I did but... you make it sound so horrible."

"I'm only trying to persuade you to see things in proper perspective, Veronica. He treated you badly, not the other way around, which means he has no rights. But a man like that thinks he's entitled to whatever he wants, and now that he's taken a fancy to Holly I wouldn't put it past him to make a claim."

"No, Jordan never wanted family ties."

"That was then. He's at the top of the tree now. He can take on a family without it tying him down at all."

"You mean... he might try to get custody of her? I don't believe it. Besides, no court would give custody to a lone father."

"Probably not, but I doubt he'd have much difficulty finding a wife somewhere. I expect he's got a dozen willing ladies. That kind always has."

"Nonsense!" But she couldn't help but remember the way Jordan had exchanged conspiratorial looks with Holly, shutting Veronica out. "It's impossible," she said firmly, trying to sound convinced.

"It is while you've got that document, plus me to look after you." He began to draw her close. "There'll be advantages to having a lawyer in the family." He laid his lips on hers, tightening his embrace. Veronica stood in his arms, longing for the old feeling of tenderness and comfortable affection, miserably aware that nothing was happening. "Come on, darling," Derek said, a touch impatiently. "You mustn't let yourself worry about things. It's a waste of time." He gave a slightly forced laugh. "The sooner we're married the better. I might have all your attention then."

"I haven't been giving you much attention, have I?" she agreed, relieved at seeing an escape. "This whole situation isn't fair to you."

"Have I ever complained? Have I said a word against you for having an illegitimate child, or for posing in the altogether? I had to put up with some very cheap jokes in the office when that poster came out, but I didn't make your life difficult about it, did I?"

Veronica paused for a moment, finally understanding something that she'd discerned only vaguely before. "No, you didn't," she conceded. "In fact, you've been very generous, Derek."

Modestly he didn't deny it. "Well, then..."

"In fact, I really don't feel I should strain your generosity any further. I should hate for you to become the butt of more cheap jokes because you'd married a woman who wasn't quite acceptable."

Derek's best friends wouldn't have called him perceptive, but the glint in Veronica's eyes was unmistakable. "Look, you're upset. I'll come back another time," he said hastily.

"No, Derek, let's settle this now. I'd rather we parted friends."

"Parted?"

"I can't marry you. I'm grateful for all the kindness you've shown me, but I'd make a very bad wife. I'm sorry if I let you believe I meant to marry you, but I've been confused."

"Are you telling me you aren't still confused?" he asked wryly.

"What do you mean?"

"You're not fooling yourself about Jordan Cavendish's intentions are you?"

"I've always seen Jordan very clearly."

"I hope so, because if you've decided to make a play for his millions, you're going to get burned."

"Derek, I think your bad angel must be working overtime today," Veronica told him crisply. "You can't open your mouth without saying something either tactless or tasteless or both. Apart from anything else, I could never marry a man who calls my daughter illegitimate.''

"But she is," he said blankly.

Veronica took a deep breath. "Only technically. And if you can't see why I find the word offensive—" She checked herself before she grew too heated. "Let's say goodbye now."

She kissed his cheek and moved back quickly before he could take hold of her. After that there was nothing for him to do but go. She stood on the step as he drove away, knowing that he hadn't understood. But she understood very little herself.

Jordan's wealth and reputation had been built on a steel-trap mind, a steady nerve and the ability to size up a situation in a flash and manipulate it to his own benefit. So it was disturbing when he realized he'd developed a tendency to act impulsively.

The sudden madness that had brought him back from Paris to rush to the hospital had been one example, and the pain of discovering Veronica being comforted by Derek had taught him a lesson very quickly—there would be no more such impulses.

Despite this resolve, he found himself driving back in the direction of Elmbridge a few hours after leaving.

It was nearly dark when he arrived, but Derek's car was nowhere in sight. He went around the side of the house to the French windows where he'd entered the previous day. The room was empty, but as he went deeper into the house he heard the sound of Holly's voice coming from upstairs, with occasional interruptions from Veronica.

FREE-GIFT COMPUTER CARD

TEAR OFF HERE AND MAIL THIS CARD TODAY!

MAIL THIS FREE-GIFT COMPUTER CARD

SILHOUETTE FREE GIFT DEPT.

to receive 4 FREE Silhouette Romances®... *PLUS* a FREE Surprise Bonus!

Use this heart to get a
FREE SURPRISE BONUS!

FREE!
AFFIX THIS
STICKER IN
SPACE AT
RIGHT

Yes! Send me 4 Free Silhouette Romances plus A Free Surprise Bonus. Then send me six new Silhouette Romances each month and bill me just $1.95 per book. No postage and handling charges. If I am not fully satisfied, I may return a shipment and cancel at any time. The 4 Free Books and Surprise Bonus remain mine to keep.

215 CIL HAXW

☐ MR.
☐ MRS.
☐ MISS

FIRST NAME | INITIAL | LAST NAME

PRINT YOUR NAME HERE FOR DATA PROCESSING (Please PRINT in ink)

ADDRESS | APT.

CITY | STATE | ZIP

Offer limited to one per household and not valid for present Romance subscribers. Prices subject to change.

FREE GIFT DEADLINE: | S | E | P | T | 3 | 0 | 1 | 9 | 8 | 8 |

TEAR OFF HERE AND MAIL THIS CARD TODAY!

DATA PROCESSING #1348
0000000000000000000
45 46 47 48 49 50 51 52 53 54 55 56
1111111111111111111
2222222222222222222

PLACE GOLD HEART HERE

to receive your **FREE** Surprise Bonus

Printed in U.S.A.

PLEASE MAIL THE ATTACHED FREE-GIFT COMPUTER CARD PROMPTLY!

NO POSTAGE NECESSARY IF MAILED IN THE UNITED STATES

APPROVED FREE-GIFT OFFER

BUSINESS REPLY CARD
FIRST CLASS   PERMIT NO. 717   BUFFALO, NY

POSTAGE WILL BE PAID BY ADDRESSEE

Silhouette Books®

901 Fuhrmann Blvd.,
P.O. Box 1867
Buffalo, NY 14240-9952

He had a sudden longing to see them together, unobserved, and moved quietly up the stairs until he came to Holly's room. The door was several inches ajar, and through the gap he could see the little girl sitting up in bed in a flannel nightgown covered with cartoon animals. The room was lit only by a small night-light that threw a soft glow onto her face.

Veronica was sitting on the edge of the bed, almost in darkness, except where the light briefly touched her red-gold hair. She was smiling tenderly as she listened to Holly's eager chatter, and it seemed to Jordan that the two of them were enveloped in the magic circle of the love uniting them.

Something contracted in his heart. It never occurred to him that he was eavesdropping. He only wanted to stay where he was, bathed in the warmth that was reaching out to him from that room. He held his breath, fearful of being discovered.

Holly was talking about her invention. "I *think* it would work," she said, furrowing her brow. "It looked terribly exciting when Jordan put all the pictures on the screen."

"You like Jordan very much, don't you?" Veronica asked hesitantly.

Holly nodded. "I like talking to him because he understands."

"What does he understand?"

"Everything," Holly said simply.

There was a silence before Veronica said, "Darling, I think it's wonderful that you and Jordan get along so well, but I don't think you should count on his coming back. He's a very busy man."

"But he can be busy here, Mommy. He showed me all his companies on his computer. It was ever so interesting."

"I'm glad, but you really shouldn't have disturbed him when he was working."

"But he didn't mind, honestly. The only time he got cross was when Derek came in."

"Why, what happened?"

"Nothing actually happened, but it was like when you see two dogs with their hackles raised. And then he went away without saying goodbye to me."

Veronica spoke quickly. "You mustn't be upset about that."

"I'm not upset—not really. But he seems sort of unhappy, as if there was no one to look after him."

"I don't think he needs anybody," Veronica said wryly. "He's very good at looking after himself."

"Then why does he look so sad?"

Veronica's answer sounded light, almost amused. "I think you're imagining that, Holly."

Jordan moved farther back into the shadows and rested his head against the wall, his heart heavy. Once there'd been someone else who'd thought he needed looking after and who'd tried to care for him. But he'd let her go, not understanding what he had, and now in her place was this wry woman who talked like a stranger.

"I'm not imagining it," Holly said indignantly. "He does seem sad, and he gives you funny looks when you're not looking at him, as though he could see something over your shoulder." She paused before asking hesitantly, "Mommy, did you know Jordan before this?"

"Yes, darling. We were friends once, but we haven't met for some time." Veronica sounded indifferently cheerful.

"But you don't like him now, do you?" the little girl persisted.

"Of course I like him."

"No, you don't. You didn't want him to stay, and when he's here you're all on edge."

"It's only that I don't want you to get too fond of him, pet. It was nice of him to come to see us, but I don't think he'll come again. There's no place in his life for us. I can't tell you how I know that, but I do."

Jordan's knuckles were white in the darkness. He pressed closer to the wall, straining to hear Holly's soft voice. At last it came. "Is he...is Jordan my father?"

The silence seemed to stretch for all eternity before Veronica answered, "We talked about your father once before, and you agreed to wait until I was ready to tell you."

"Yes, but...is he?" Holly repeated eagerly.

"Darling, please be patient. Trust me. I'll tell you everything one day. In the meantime, I don't want you to think of him as your father."

Jordan's muscles were aching from the effort of holding himself still. He let out his breath slowly and silently and began to edge toward the top of the stairs, one careful step at a time. He descended soundlessly and in another minute had left the house, without Veronica ever having known he was there.

For the first part of the journey home he raged, calling himself a fool. For the second part his cool brain took over, calculating possibilities, devising ways and means. By the time he reached his apartment his plan was laid down to the last detail.

He poured himself a stiff drink while he ran over the details one last time, until he was satisfied that he'd allowed for everything. It was time to set the first stage in motion.

He picked up the phone and called Lorrayne.

Chapter Seven

Veronica had found a friend in Mrs. Hendricks. She was a woman of few words, but those words were usually to the point. She'd looked Jordan up and down and said nothing, but Veronica had a feeling she'd sized up the situation. And it was Mrs. Hendricks who gave her the clue to Derek's behavior.

"He reminds me of my Alfred," she said, referring to her late and apparently unlamented spouse. "He could be as nice as pie if I was sick. He'd bring me tea, speak to me kindly, nothing was too much trouble. Then as soon as I was on my feet he'd start shouting at me again."

"But I wasn't sick," Veronica protested.

"You were having a bad time, though, weren't you?" Mrs. Hendricks observed. "Now he reckons you're all right, so he can take off the kid gloves. You're lucky you found out in time. If you ask me the other one's worth ten of him."

"'The other one' won't be coming back, Mrs. Hendricks," Veronica said firmly.

Mrs. Hendricks responded with a grunt, to which, Veronica discovered, there was no possible answer.

The car and driver that Jordan had hired to take them to the country turned up again promptly every week to convey Holly to the Jameson Clinic for her checkup. By now she and Dr. Weston were old friends and chatted easily. Beneath his ready cheerfulness the surgeon was a brilliant man whose eyes missed nothing. When he pronounced Holly improving fast Veronica relaxed visibly.

Before going home Holly liked to browse in the shops, especially those that specialized in computers. Veronica viewed this interest with apprehension because she was sure it was Jordan's machine that had started Holly down this road, but she hadn't the heart to draw her away.

The first time they went to town Veronica said, when they'd finished browsing, "If I don't have some tea soon I'll pass out for sure."

Holly pointed to a building nearby. "Let's go in there."

"Darling, that's the Ritz!" Veronica exclaimed faintly.

"But people have tea there," Holly insisted. "You can see them through the window."

Veronica gulped at the thought of tea in one of the most luxurious hotels in London, but she was too thirsty to worry. And when they'd trudged inside and seated themselves in the tearoom she found that the prices came more within her budget than she'd thought. Holly sighed ecstatically over the cream cakes, and embarked on a demonstration of how much her appetite had improved. After that, tea at the Ritz became an indispensable part of their trips.

Veronica heard no more from Jordan after she'd ordered him out of the house. She tried to talk herself into a sensible frame of mind, but she was disappointed at his silence. It was hurtful to have parted bad friends, even if he *had* been unreasonable. And she had an irrational desire to tell him she wasn't going to marry Derek.

A few days after Jordan's visit she and Holly went to town again, and Dr. Weston told them that Holly would only need a few more checkups.

They celebrated over éclairs at the Ritz, with Holly chattering nonstop. She had a fund of stories about her time in the hospital, and Veronica listened, laughing at the anecdotes.

Then the smile froze on her face as she looked over Holly's head at the entrance to the bar. Through the archway she could see Jordan seated at a table talking to a slender and extremely beautiful chestnut-haired woman, dressed in the latest fashion. Even from across the room Veronica could see that her appearance had the kind of attention only money could procure. She turned her head and Veronica recognized Lorrayne Haslam.

She told herself she had no business to be agitated. She'd sent Jordan away, telling him their passion meant nothing. He had every right to take her at her word and return to his "constant companion." But it hurt to see him with this poised woman, who leaned close as if she owned him, and smiled. There was something knowing and intimate in that smile that shot pain through Veronica's heart.

She tried to tear her glance away, but she couldn't help watching Jordan's face to see how he looked at the woman. Did he love her? Was there desire in his glance, the kind of desire that Veronica could inspire in him? But the bar was dimly lit and it was hard to make out details. He was leaning back, talking, occasionally smiling, but she couldn't see his eyes.

The woman laughed, and there was a sudden moment when all the noise seemed to cease at once, long enough for Veronica to hear her say, "Oh, darling, really..." before the noise closed in again.

A waitress appeared at her table. "Will that be all, madam?"

"No, I'd like another pot of tea, please."

She shouldn't have done that. She should have bundled Holly up and left right then. But she couldn't tear herself away from the sight of him looking so at ease in this woman's company. She smiled at something Holly said, but jealousy was gnawing at her painfully.

Then she saw Jordan reach into his briefcase and take out a long, flat box, which he handed to Lorrayne. She opened it and Veronica just caught sight of a magnificent diamond necklace. Veronica took a deep, painful breath. Even a man of Jordan's wealth wouldn't give such a thing lightly.

Lorrayne exclaimed in delight and reached across the table to touch Jordan's cheek, which seemed to make him uncomfortable. He removed her hand, patting it and laughing awkwardly. Veronica reflected that a woman had to be very sure of her position with a man to risk embarrassing him in public. She turned her head so that she couldn't see them.

The fresh pot of tea was served, and she concentrated on pouring it. When she allowed herself to look up again, Jordan and Lorrayne were rising. As they emerged through the archway into the lobby where tea was served, Jordan glanced around casually, and Veronica knew by the way he stiffened that he'd seen her. For a moment their eyes met. Even at this distance she could see his dismay. His lips tightened, and for a moment he showed an indecision rare in him. Then he put his hand under Lorrayne's arm and began to lead her out.

He was forestalled by Holly who followed her mother's gaze and brightened when she saw Jordan. She was out of her chair in a flash, avoiding Veronica's restraining hand to scamper across to him. Veronica held her breath, praying he wouldn't show his displeasure with the child for intruding on him. To her relief he smiled at Holly, but his manner was constrained.

Veronica hurried over and Jordan greeted her politely, but still she was sure he would have liked to avoid this meeting. "Veronica, I'd like you to meet Lorrayne Haslam," he said. "Lorrayne, this is Veronica Grant, and her daughter, Holly."

The two women gave each other a nod and a half smile. Holly put out her hand to Lorrayne and said "How do you do?" Lorrayne ignored the hand and leaned down to smother Holly in a perfumed embrace. "What a dear little girl," she said.

Holly squirmed, her eyes hostile. Only her beautiful manners prevented her from breaking free. Lorrayne straightened and smiled at Jordan. "You didn't tell me you had such charming friends," she said. "Let's all sit down for a few minutes."

Courtesy demanded that Jordan and Veronica pretend to be delighted. The only person really pleased was Holly, who promptly claimed a seat next to Jordan. Lorrayne coolly seated herself on his other side, leaving Veronica, sitting on the far side of the low table, with no choice but to watch Jordan's face. It seemed to her jealous fancy that he avoided looking at her. "What have you been doing with yourself?" he asked Holly.

"I've been to the hospital for a checkup, and the doctor says I only need to go a couple more times," she told him happily.

"Oh, dear, have you been ill?" Lorrayne asked in a cooing voice. "That's very sad."

"I had an operation on my heart, but I'm quite better now, thank you very much," Holly said.

"You're very brave," Lorrayne said, beaming at her. "But it must have been a terrible experience for you."

"No, it wasn't, it was fun," Holly said firmly. "I don't think it was much fun for George, though. He was the orderly," she added to Veronica.

"The one you apologized to?"

"That's right."

"What had you done?" Jordan demanded.

"He was pushing me down a corridor in a wheelchair, and he met this nurse. She was ever so pretty and I think that's why he forgot me for a moment." Holly chuckled. "And when he looked back I wasn't there."

"Holly!" Veronica exclaimed in dismay.

"I'd slipped into the laundry room. It took them ten minutes to find me and George was wailing, 'I'll do time for that child! See if I don't!'"

Jordan laughed. "I'll bet they were glad when you left," he said, grinning.

"They were," Holly agreed gleefully.

Veronica tried to keep a straight face, but her lips trembled. Involuntarily she met Jordan's eye, and for a moment their shared understanding flashed between them, excluding Lorrayne, who had leisure to look narrowly from one to the other.

"It was very naughty of you," Veronica declared, but her tone wasn't quite steady.

"Yes," the child agreed, not in the least abashed. She added happily, "George said if I'd stayed any longer he'd have had a nervous breakdown."

"Holly," Veronica chided her gently, "stop showing off."

"Oh, leave her alone," Lorrayne purred. "She's such a darling."

Holly looked less than overwhelmed by this tribute. She favored Lorrayne with a smile of such perfect, blank courtesy that Veronica stiffened, knowing that her daughter had taken one of her rare but intense dislikes. Phrases from a profile of Lorrayne she'd read in a glossy magazine floated through her head. "A socialite who really knows how to have fun...colorful friends, a hard-living, hard-playing crowd..."

Lorrayne was looking at Holly in a speculative way that made Veronica want to seize her child and run a mile in the opposite direction, but Holly was oblivious. She turned to Jordan and said reproachfully, "You haven't been to Elmbridge for ages."

"I'll be down soon," he promised.

"Elmbridge," Lorrayne echoed. "What a charming name!"

"It's our home in the country," Holly informed her politely. "Only it's not really ours. It belongs to a friend of Mommy's and we're just staying there."

"What a nice friend," Lorrayne said. "You must be very fond of him."

"I don't know if it's a him or a her, because Mommy won't tell me who it is," Holly informed her.

"But how unkind of Mommy," Lorrayne cried playfully.

"It doesn't seem of the slightest importance to me," Veronica said crisply.

"Not the slightest," Jordan agreed. "Shall we drop the subject?" His tone was pleasant, but to Veronica's jealous eyes it was clear he was on hot coals. He ruffled Holly's hair. "I'll be down when I can."

"You're honored," Lorrayne told Holly. "Jordan's usually much too busy to make social calls."

"That's what Mommy says," Holly agreed. "But you really will come, won't you?" she pressed Jordan.

"Promise." Before Holly could say any more he distracted her quickly. "How about an ice cream?"

"Yes, please."

He called the waitress, and he and Holly plunged into an animated discussion of the merits of strawberry ripple and chocolate fudge. Lorrayne turned to Veronica and gave her a smile uncannily reminiscent of the Cheshire cat's. "You must know Jordan very well if you've already learned not to rely on him," she said sweetly.

Veronica smiled but remained silent. She wasn't going to give Lorrayne the satisfaction of drawing her out. Lorrayne's mouth tightened a little as she realized she wasn't going to get an answer. Her eyes swept over Veronica, seeming to take in her youth and beauty, and she nodded as if she'd only just understood something. "You must forgive my staring at you," she said charmingly, "but I can't believe someone so young is that little girl's mother. Or did I hear it wrong? Perhaps you're her older sister?"

"I'm Holly's mother," Veronica said firmly.

"But you must have been little more than a child yourself when you had her."

"I was fairly young," Veronica agreed, returning fire with fire, "but I believe that's the best time to have children, don't you?"

"I wouldn't know. I haven't been as lucky as you. Or do I mean as clever? You and your husband obviously had it all worked out in advance."

Lorrayne was too intelligent to let her eyes linger on Veronica's bare left hand, but the message was plain as day. Veronica smiled back, giving nothing away. "The best laid plans can go awry," she observed affably. "Don't you find that?"

Lorrayne gave her rich, saccharine chuckle. "I do indeed. But if that little pet was a 'mistake' she must be the *shrewdest* mistake you ever made." She lingered a little to let her meaning sink in, before going on. "So bright and charming. But should the poor little thing be bouncing around quite so much if she's recently had major surgery?"

"Holly wouldn't thank you for calling her a poor little thing," Veronica retorted crisply. "According to the doctor she's perfectly well. It's good for her to be lively."

"And of course she has all that lovely countryside," Lorrayne purred. "How lucky you are to have a friend with a country house to put at your disposal.

But then, I'm sure you're always very lucky in your friends."

The insult behind the softly spoken words was so unmistakable that Veronica had no hesitation in responding in kind. "I *am* lucky in my friends. They're loyal and honest, and they don't believe that money buys everything, something that can't be said for all friends—can it?"

Lorrayne's eyes hardened, though her mouth retained the smile she'd fixed in place. "I see," she murmured. "Yes, I see." And something in her tone made a shiver go up Veronica's spine.

"Holly," she said, "don't be too long over that ice cream. We have to be going soon."

Jordan had been talking to Holly, but he looked up when he heard the edge in Veronica's voice and seized her cue. "We have to be going *now*," he said firmly. "Will you forgive us if we rush away before you've finished?"

"Oh, but surely..." Lorrayne laughingly protested, but Jordan's arm was under her elbow and he was helping her insistently to her feet.

Veronica could see he was determined to bring this disastrous meeting to an end, and she herself would be glad to have it over. "Of course I know how busy you are," she murmured.

Lorrayne smothered Holly in another scented embrace before allowing Jordan to lead her away. At the exit she turned and waved to them. Holly watched them go, her eyes troubled. "Mommy," she said at last, "I don't like that lady. She called me 'a dear little girl.'"

"I know, darling," Veronica said grimly. "I heard her."

* * *

One morning Holly asked, "Mommy, is Jordan a bandit?"

After a brief moment's surprise, Veronica recovered and said wryly, "I'm sure some of his opponents would say that's a very good description. Why?"

"Because the newspaper says he 'mounted a dawn raid' on somebody called Garvin Redway." She pushed the paper over the breakfast table, and Veronica saw a picture of Jordan beneath the headline, "Cavenidish takes Redway by surprise."

The text continued, "Tycoon Jordan Cavendish signified to finance watchers that he's intensifying his battle with rival Garvin Redway by mounting a dawn raid on Redway shares. The surprise move brought him within a hair's breadth of the stake needed to take control of the giant corporation and become the most powerful..." Veronica skimmed through the rest.

"I don't think he actually went in there brandishing a six-shooter," she said. "Although it must have felt like it to them. I believe a dawn raid is a way of buying shares."

Holly's face fell momentarily, but she brightened again. "I'll have to ask him," she said.

"Holly, please don't expect him back," Veronica begged uneasily. "If he's starting a fight it'll take all his attention."

"But he'll still come and see us."

"Darling, I wish you wouldn't count on that."

"But he will. He said he would. He's my friend," Holly insisted.

It was two weeks since they'd encountered Jordan with Lorrayne, and they'd heard no more from him. Veronica was torn between two fears—that Holly had become too attached to a man whose interest in her would be fleeting at best, and that Jordan's interest would grow and he'd make a permanent claim. It was all too clear that such a claim wouldn't include her, and she was resolved to fight it. Jordan could make Holly an heiress, but he would also give her Lorrayne Haslam as a mother, and Veronica would never allow that affected, hard-living woman to take over her vulnerable little daughter.

To Veronica's dismay Holly began to read the papers eagerly whenever Jordan's name was mentioned. Although much of it went over her head she understood far more than Veronica had expected and followed the battle with enthusiasm. It was clear to her mother that she'd inherited Jordan's brains without Jordan's hard, suspicious character.

But then she remembered the stories he'd once told her of his life in the institution, and she wondered what kind of man he could have been if he'd known a warm and loving home.

She, too, began to follow the takeover battle, and what she learned was shocking. She'd known Jordan was extremely rich, but not the full extent of his wealth. Now the financial journalists were dissecting him, speaking of tens of millions of pounds.

She was horrified as she remembered Derek's casual reference to "making a play for his millions." She could see now why Jordan had so easily thought the same thing.

Luckily Holly's ninth birthday was drawing near, and as the days slipped past, planning absorbed all her attention. Mrs. Hendricks had made and iced a cake to be decorated with nine candles, and Veronica had scoured the shops for books that might challenge

Holly's precocious intelligence. For good measure she threw in a chemistry set that she knew would appeal to her practical daughter.

When her birthday arrived Holly awoke at six-thirty in the morning and thereafter looked in on her mother at ten-minute intervals. At seven-thirty Veronica gave in and sleepily swung her legs out of bed. She was immediately set on by a tousled, squealing, wriggling creature who seemed intent on tickling her to death. She responded in kind, and they wrestled breathlessly until they fell off the bed with a thump.

"Let's call that a draw," Veronica pleaded, warding off another attack.

"Draw nothing! I beat you," Holly asserted indignantly.

"All right, you beat me. I surrender." She yawned. "You might have waited until I was properly awake, you little wretch."

"I'm nine today," Holly announced proudly.

"As if that was an excuse for knocking me black and blue," Veronica complained comically.

Holly seized her hand and pulled her downstairs just in time for the arrival of the mail. She opened all her cards excitedly and set them up on the mantelpiece. It seemed to Veronica that a faint shadow crossed her face as she realized that there was an omission, but Veronica couldn't tell Holly that her birthday was a delicate subject with Jordan.

Over breakfast she asked, "How would you like to go to Moncastle today? It's a stately home—" Holly's mouth went down at the corners "—and it has a collection of vintage cars," Veronica finished, laughing as the child's face was transformed.

While Holly bounded upstairs to get ready Veronica called a taxi and followed her up. She chose a pair of olive-green corduroy trousers and added a yellow shirt, fixing her hair back with a scarf of the same color. She was tying the knot when she heard a car approaching the house. "Holly," she called. "Taxi!"

The next moment she heard a shriek of delight, followed by the pounding of feet down the stairs. With a sudden foreboding she went to a landing window that overlooked the front of the house. Then her heart lurched with a mixture of fear, pain and indescribable joy.

It was Jordan.

Chapter Eight

As Veronica watched, Holly hurtled out the front door and raced toward the car. Jordan braked as soon as he saw her, and Holly clambered in and flung her arms around his neck. Although it was too far away to be sure, Veronica thought she saw Jordan slip an arm around Holly and hug her while he put the car in gear with his other hand.

Veronica reached the front step just as Jordan got out of the car. He was dressed casually in a short-sleeved polo shirt, and looked younger and more relaxed than she'd seen him since the night of their reunion. He stood there, smiling at Veronica, while her heart turned over despite herself, and she tried to decide if she was glad or sorry that he was here.

"Sorry to descend on you unannounced," he said, "but I want to ask Holly to do me a favor."

"What kind of a favor?" Veronica asked.

He gestured to the car with his head. "It's about something I've got in there. Wait and I'll bring it in."

He reached into the back seat and took out a large box, which he carried into the house and set down on a table in the living room. Holly bounced after him and hung around eagerly as he began to unpack the contents, talking as he did. "I had a consignment of these delivered to my office, but my secretary ordered one too many. Sending it back would involve more paperwork than it's worth, so I thought if Holly could find a corner for it, that would save me a lot of trouble."

With a flourish he tossed away the last piece of packing to reveal a personal computer. Holly drew in a long breath and then became totally silent, while her eyes told of her wonder. "You mean... it's for me?" she asked when she'd recovered her voice.

"For you and no one else, if you want it. Of course if it's too much trouble..." Laughing, he pretended to start repacking, but Holly reached out quickly to stop him.

"It isn't, it isn't," she said breathlessly. "Oh, Jordan, thank you." She began to touch the keyboard with loving fingers. "It's different from yours," she said with fascination.

"The one you saw was only a portable machine. This is far more powerful. It can do all sorts of things you wouldn't even dream of."

"And you're going to stay and show me how to work it? Oh, please stay. And you can have some of my birthday cake."

"You mean it's your birthday?" Jordan asked, apparently astonished. "What a lucky chance that I turned up today."

Holly giggled. "It's not a chance. You knew it was my birthday."

"No, how could I? You only told me you were going to be nine soon. You didn't say it would be today."

"But I'll bet you could find out," Holly insisted. "I'll bet you could find out anything you wanted to."

He cocked his head to observe her. "How?" he challenged.

She considered. "You could...mount a dawn raid," she announced triumphantly.

Jordan shouted with laughter. "So you are a budding tycoon," he said. "The sooner I teach you to work this thing the better."

Veronica had listened to this exchange, a prey to mixed feelings. It was briefly hurtful to know that Jordan's arrival could make Holly forget her so completely.

But then she looked at her child's face, radiant with joy, and she knew that if Jordan hadn't come here today she would never have forgiven him.

She's his daughter in spirit as well as in the flesh, Veronica thought, so they naturally turn to each other. How long before he sees it? Or has he seen it already?

"The taxi's arrived," Mrs. Hendricks said, looking around the door.

Holly's hand flew to her mouth and Jordan looked questioningly. "We were just on our way out to see a collection of vintage cars," Veronica explained.

"But we could go another day, couldn't we, Mommy?" Holly pleaded. Then, afraid she was being selfish, she added, "Unless you were looking forward to it very much."

"We'll go another time," she said, smiling. "This is your day."

Jordan nodded. "Nine's a milestone," he said to Holly. "It's your last birthday in single figures."

Veronica departed to pay the taxi driver for his trouble. When she returned Jordan was fitting together the various parts of the computer while Holly attached a plug to the cable, with an expression of fierce concentration. "Is it all right for her to do that?" Jordan asked in an undertone.

"She's better at mechanical things than I am," Veronica told him. "And probably better than you, too."

He grinned. "Anyone's better than I am."

"What are you up to, Jordan?"

"Up to?" he asked innocently. "Me?"

"Don't ask me to believe that the superefficient Kate Adams made a mistake, or that you'd have cared how much paperwork was involved in resolving it."

He grinned sheepishly. "How did she know what a dawn raid is?"

"She doesn't. She's going to ask you. She's been following your progress in the papers, and now she has a whole list of things she wants to know."

"Good for her," he said admiringly. "Have you been following my progress, too?"

"One of us is quite enough," Veronica informed him tartly. "And how come you could take a day off from all this fighting?"

He shrugged. "The worst's over. I'm going to win. But I have the feeling you're not a hundred percent pleased to see me. Is Derek going to appear from behind the drapes? Should I be shaking in my shoes?"

His playful words brought back Derek's claim to have "disconcerted" Jordan, and she couldn't suppress a choke of laughter. "What's so funny?" he demanded, trying to catch her eye as she looked away from him.

"Nothing," she said hastily. "Forget it."

"Where *is* Derek? Shouldn't he be here?"

"He's not coming. That's all I'm going to say."

"That's really all you need to say," he commented shrewdly. "All right, you can tell me later."

"If I decide to tell you anything at all, which is extremely unlikely, considering it's none of your business," she informed him spiritedly.

"Hmm. Obviously Holly's going to make me more welcome than you are."

"You've made Holly's day," she admitted. "I'm grateful that you took the trouble to come. Let's leave it at that, Jordan."

"I didn't really come to see Holly," he said so softly that she barely heard him. "I came to see you." His eyes swept over her and he added, "I think I came just to see you in that shade of buttercup yellow. I'm glad you're still taking my advice."

"Advice?"

"I persuaded you to start wearing that shade. You thought it would be too much with your hair, but I made you try it, and you said I was right."

It came back to her then, how imaginative he'd sometimes been, and how strangely it had mixed with his hardheaded, practical side. She'd forgotten about his determination to see her in yellow. But he hadn't. He nodded conspiratorially, and she searched his face, wondering what to say. She could feel her heart beating strongly.

"It's ready," Holly called, and they came back to the present. Jordan went to the table where the computer was set up, and switched it on. Holly's childishness seemed to drop away from her as he instructed her in its use, and she became an earnest student, absorbed in serious matters.

But when she got the hang of the graphics she became a child again, playing gleefully with colors and shapes. She was endlessly inventive. "She'll be writing her own programs before you know it," Jordan told Veronica.

Then Holly had to show her mother her new treasure and proudly demonstrate how it worked. She doubled up with laughter over Veronica's mistakes, and Jordan joined in. A stranger who chanced to look through the window would have smiled at such an obviously happy, united family.

They had a picnic lunch in the garden and as soon as possible Holly departed, clutching a cheese roll in one hand and a glass of milk in the other. A minute later they heard her hard at work tapping the keyboard. Jordan grinned. "She's like a terrier with something between its teeth," he said. "She doesn't let go."

He rose, taking Veronica's hand. "Let's take a walk," he said.

She tried to hold back, determined to be cautious, but he wouldn't be refused, and she found herself drawn through the garden, his arm around her shoulders. "Are you sorry I came?" he asked.

Now was the right moment for her to say something. She could teasingly say, Does Lorrayne know you're here? or smile and say lightly, I'm surprised Lorrayne lets you out without her. Her throat was dry as she tried to summon a careless laugh.

Then she looked into his face, and all the words left her, taking her doubts with them. Jordan could be ruthless but not dishonest, harsh but not devious. It was his stark honesty that had once driven them apart because he wouldn't pretend there was a place in his life for her when there wasn't. The unanswered questions tormented her when he was away, but here in the circle of his arm, his candid eyes gazing into hers, they ceased to matter.

"No, I'm not sorry," she said.

There was a sudden tension in his face, and he stepped toward her but then stopped and looked back at the house, realizing how conspicuous they were. He began to guide her in the direction of the wood. "It would have broken Holly's heart if you hadn't been here," Veronica added. "Thanks to you, the world's beginning for her again."

"Nine years after it began for the first time," he said. "I checked her birth certificate in the Public Records Office. She was born nine months and two weeks after we last saw each other. I didn't have to look that date up. I never forgot it," he added quietly.

"It's that two weeks that bothers you, isn't it?"

"Of course it does. I can't get past the thought that she was conceived two weeks after our last meeting." Veronica was silent. "Say something," he commanded urgently.

"Anything I could say would infringe on the terms of our agreement."

"To hell with the damned agreement," he said, scowling. "Say it, whatever it is."

"All right. Holly was a first baby. They often arrive late."

"As late as that?"

"Two weeks isn't exceptional with a first child."

"You'd know more about that than I would," Jordan said, adding quietly, "there've been no babies in my life."

He spoke almost to himself, and Veronica fancied she detected a hint of reproach in his voice.

They'd reached the limit of the cultivated part of the garden and passed on into the little wood. The sun had climbed to its height and streamed down through the leafy branches in straight lines of dazzling light. Beyond them everything seemed faded, as though the world outside this small circle was dissolving.

Inside it she was aware of a heightened reality. The scents of summer filled her nostrils, dizzying her with images of ripeness and fulfillment. Her senses leaped at the nearness of the man walking beside her, and looking up, she could see how the fine hairs on his face caught the sun, surrounding him in a golden glow.

He'd spoken words of rejection, yet his arm was around her, holding her so tightly against his side as they walked that she could feel his movements against her own. "Where have you been these ten years?" he asked.

"I went home to my parents to have Holly. I was able to stay there for a while afterward and just enjoy her."

"You never wanted to be tied down with babies," he reminded her.

"That was before I had one. It didn't feel like being tied down, it felt..."

It had felt like still having some part of him there. The baby's warmth and sweetness had filled her empty arms and her emptier heart, until they weren't empty any longer, but full to overflowing with love and joy.

She'd loved Holly for her own sake, but also for the man who fathered her.

"It felt wonderful," she finished simply.

He looked down at her, but he was ten inches taller and couldn't see her face properly. He put his fingers under her chin and tilted it up. Her eyes met his, clear and beautiful as nothing in his life had been since the loss of her. "Go on," he urged.

"I stayed with my parents for two years," she said slowly. "Then I started acting again, leaving Holly with them while I was away... and after that—" Her heart was pounding as his head blotted out the sun and his lips touched hers.

At their last meeting he'd kissed her with angry passion, resenting the feelings she could arouse in him even while he yielded to them. Now he kissed her as he had on the night of their reunion, tenderly and with wonder. The movements of his mouth were gentle, caressing her with subtle persuasion, but cautiously, as though he was afraid the spell might break.

He drew back slightly and brushed her face with his fingertips. He seemed puzzled, as if something had taken him by surprise, and the answering look in her eyes told him it was the same with her. After a moment they walked on, as if sensing that the time wasn't right, but their arms were still entwined.

"I'd like to know everything," he persisted. "I wish you'd—" He checked himself in frustration. Their written agreement turned the lightest utterance into a two-edged sword, and he was more at home with directness than subtlety. "I wish you'd written to me and asked for help," he finished awkwardly.

"But how could I ask you for help in providing for another man's child?" she challenged him.

"Veronica." He growled her name in a way that was part warning not to tread on dangerous territory and part plea not to spoil the moment. "We'd been good friends, and I don't like to think of how poor you must have been."

"Only in money," she said, with a smile that shut him out, even while she looked at him. "I was so blessed in everything else. Holly was a gorgeous baby. She's lean and wiry now, but in those days she was round and rosy cheeked. She was always chuckling. I don't think there was ever such a merry child."

"Your daughter," he mused. "You were just like that, as though all of life was your own private joke. The first time you ever spoke to me, you urged me to laugh."

"Did I?"

"I was in the office of the theater manager, doing the books. You dashed in and collided with some shelves that were stacked with files, and the whole lot came down on you. The manager roared with laughter. I was furious with him for finding it funny, but you were laughing, too. I helped to dust you off and you looked up at me and said, 'It's not a crime to laugh.'"

Her own recollections of those days were as clear as his—but about other things, reflecting their different priorities. She remembered Jordan himself, dour, nervous and unexpectedly thin-skinned. She recalled her young, passionate love for him, and her joy at the awkward intensity with which he sometimes turned to her. But detailed incidents stood out less sharply in her mind, whereas Jordan's computerlike memory seized solid facts.

"Was that our very first meeting?" she asked. "Didn't we meet at a backstage party?"

"No, it was in the office," he said firmly. "But I'm not surprised it doesn't stand out as a big event in your life. You didn't notice me at first, you were too busy adoring Emeric Laidley."

"Who?"

"He was the leading man. You can say 'Who?' now but then you were entangled in the deepest case of puppy love I've ever seen. Actually he was an egotistical, Brylcreemed, corsetted pip-squeak, long past what little best he ever had. He used to take advantage of you, saying, 'Shall we just go through our scene again?' You only had five minutes with him and he rehearsed it into the ground just to keep getting his arm around your waist. If you hadn't been so young and innocent you'd have seen right through him."

Veronica smothered a laugh. She's seen through Emeric Laidley without trouble, but she'd been trying to make Jordan jealous. It was delightful to learn, after all this time, that she'd succeeded. "What were you doing hanging around the theater when you should have been studying?" she teased.

"Someone had to protect you from that disgusting old Romeo."

"Oh, I see. You were just being a Dutch uncle." She chuckled at the memory. "You didn't look like one. Most of the time you looked like a fugitive from a chain gang."

"That was because I had my hair cut extra short to save visits to the barber. Plus, of course, the time you nearly scalped me."

"I was only trying to help. You complained how much a haircut cost, so I thought I'd save you the price. You weren't a bit grateful."

"Grateful?" he echoed, outraged. "Who cut my ear?"

"Who called me a birdbrain?"

"Who deserved it?" He grinned and rested his cheek on the top of her head. "We were mad," he said longingly.

"*You* were mad," she said, remembering another grievance. "Who worked out a mathematically infallible method of backing horses that made us bankrupt?"

"Who wanted me to try it again?"

"Well, it might have been worth it. We *did* have one winner." She dug him in the ribs. "Yes, and who picked the horse?"

"Who lost the ticket before we could claim our winnings?"

"Who never let me forget it?"

"Who told me she could handle the taxman?" Jordan demanded, "and who did she yell for to come and help her out of the mess?"

"Who was always lecturing me about financial responsibility, and then had to get me to spin a sob story to his landlady?"

"Who went without lunches for a week to buy you that crystal statuette?"

"Who dropped it?"

When their mirth subsided, Jordan kissed the top of her head. They'd reached the stream where there was a patch of mossy ground. He pulled her down and they lay together looking up at the trees, listening to the faint trickling of the water over stones. "How young we were," he said regretfully. "Whatever happened to us?"

"We grew more responsible," she said with a sigh. "Life changed, and we changed."

"And we lost so much. I never made silly jokes with anyone else but you, Ronnie. Meeting you was like having a window thrown open to let in the sun. Sunlight followed you everywhere. I used to watch you, trying to discover what gave you such joy, so that I could share your secret."

The joy had come from loving him. It had filled her life with radiance then and now it did so again, but he was still blind. "Did you ever find the secret?" she asked longingly.

"Only with you. You lit up the dark corners inside me. Apart from your light it was pretty bleak in there." He paused and Veronica lay still, listening to the beating of his heart close to her ear. After a long time he said quietly, "Then you weren't there anymore, and the darkness closed in again."

She lifted her head and searched his face, finding uncertainty, fear and hope. She noted, too, the troubled look in his eyes and she reached out to touch his cheek. He seemed to hold his breath as she stroked him gently with her fingertips. She never knew whether he lowered his head or she drew it to her, but her arm was around his neck and his lips were on hers and the world was spinning dizzily around her.

He kissed her hungrily, like a man whose heart had been empty too long, a man who was desperate to find everything in one woman. Veronica clung to him, feeling all sadness leave her, knowing she'd never stopped longing to be in his arms again. When she was seventeen her heart had been wise, knowing instinctively that this was the man she belonged to. Everything since then, tears and joy, and all she'd learned from her life had only brought her back to the same place.

"I never forgot you," he murmured as his lips caressed hers. "You were always there, haunting me, reminding me of what I'd lost because I hadn't understood... until it was too late...."

His embrace tightened before she could answer. The movements of his lips were becoming more purposeful, coaxing, demanding. Delight coursed through her as she felt the firm tip of his tongue trace the outline of her full, soft mouth, lingering over the deep, sensual curve of her lower lip. She parted her lips slightly, trying to catch his tongue and take it inside her mouth, but he eluded her playfully, assaulting her lips with small flickering motions that made her gasp with pleasure.

The sound seemed to be a signal to him. He smothered her mouth with his own and his tongue invaded her, sending her into a spiral of delight. All her senses were alive to him, every inch of her aching to feel his touch, her skin quivering with sweet anticipation.

He pulled away and raised himself on his elbows, looking down at her as she lay with her wonderful hair fanned out over the leaves. Her skin was a light golden color, and the light streaming from above deepened its warm hue. She was part of summer. Like her surroundings she was young and beautiful and full of the promise of life renewed; Demeter, goddess of corn, bringer of fruitfulness. Jordan couldn't have expressed it like that but he knew that a spring had burst forth inside him, making green what had been arid, giving beauty where before there'd been only barrenness. He didn't understand it, but he knew it all came from this golden woman he held in his arms.

He groaned suddenly and buried his face against her breasts, revelling in their ripe fullness, the soft warmth beneath his cheek. At once he felt her hands meet behind his head, drawing him closer in an age-old gesture of acceptance. It seemed to him that there was all a man could want in that gesture, and the strain began to slip away from his mind and heart and body, leaving nothing behind but the awareness of her. She claimed his senses as she'd claimed his dreams, and there was nothing in the world but her.

The soft seductiveness of her body beneath his drove him to madness. If she was telling the truth he'd once known that body. Her perfect silky skin had lain against his own, inflaming him to passion; her sweet warmth had enclosed him in a taking and giving that must have been the most perfect any man ever knew. Yet he remembered nothing.

He caressed her urgently, trying to bring back what was lost, but the girl of those days was gone forever. There was only the woman now, looking up at him from ecstatic eyes, her lips forming his name soundlessly. A calm seemed to fall over him, and he bent his head to rest his lips against the base of her throat, revelling in the smell of summer that pervaded her.

He felt her flesh quicken in response, become alive under his kiss. With infinite slowness he brought his kisses lower until he pressed his lips against the swell of her breasts, and waited there, his heart pounding.

Veronica lay still, not daring to move in case the spell should break. The touch of his mouth was inexpressibly lovely, a promise of passion and tenderness. All the love she felt for him welled up in her, almost more than she could bear. There was no pain or sadness now, only love for this one man whose child she'd borne and who was all the world to her. "Jordan..." she whispered longingly, "Jordan..."

He raised his head and his eyes shone into hers. Each read in the other's face the joy of rediscovery. Nothing mattered anymore but their two selves and what they could offer each other. Veronica started to whisper his name again, but then something halted her with the word half spoken.

In the distance she'd heard a cry, and even while her heart yearned toward her lover she knew that cry had come from the one person on earth who could make her turn from him.

"Mommy, *Mommy*!" Holly's voice came from beyond the wood, growing sharper, more frantic, changing direction every second as though its owner was running around in a desperate search. "Mommy... Jordan... quick, oh, come quickly *please*!"

Chapter Nine

At the sound of Holly's frantic voice all Veronica's nightmares rushed together and made her jerk up, thrusting Jordan aside. "Oh, God, what's happened to her?" she cried. "She must be ill again."

"She can't be—" Jordan started to say.

"Don't say that!" she flashed at him. "You don't know—" She jumped to her feet and dashed off without saying more. Her heart was pounding with terror as she fled through the trees, stumbling in the undergrowth, praying frantically until at last she found Holly running down a rough path, crying urgently, "Mommy... Jordan—"

"Darling, what is it?" Veronica dropped to her knees and stared into Holly's face. "Tell me quickly. Are you ill?"

Holly shook her head vigorously and choked back a sob, then spoke to Jordan who'd come up behind Veronica. "I've broken it," she wailed.

"Broken what?" he asked.

"The machine. It won't work anymore. It's gone dead. I've broken it, but I didn't mean to, honestly..." She hiccuped forlornly.

Veronica sat back on her heels and gave a long ragged sigh as her heart slowed to its normal beat. "Is that all that's wrong?" she demanded.

"Mommy, it's *broken*," Holly repeated, baffled by her mother's incomprehension of the tragedy.

Jordan passed a hand over his eyes. "I don't suppose it is," he said. "You probably just touched the wrong button. Shall I come and make it work for you again?"

"Yes, please." Holly's tears dried like magic, and she scampered back across the lawn, pausing briefly to call pleadingly, "Hurry up!"

Veronica was still kneeling where she'd dropped on the path. She was shaking all over and knew she didn't have the strength to get up. Jordan leaned down and pulled her gently to her feet. "Hey, come on," he urged. "It's all over. There was no reason to panic. I was trying to say that she couldn't be ill because if she was Mrs. Hendricks would have come for us, not Holly herself."

"I know," she said weakly. "But when I heard her cry out like that I felt so guilty for leaving her alone—"

"But we didn't leave her alone," he pointed out. "Mrs. Hendricks was there—"

"For pity's sake, will you stop being so rational?" she cried, her nerves at breaking point. "I can't be rational about Holly. For a moment it was as though the last few months had come back...." Shudders possessed her, and she turned away from him, clenching and unclenching her hands nervously. "I couldn't bear it again," she whispered.

Her run had left her hair tousled. Jordan turned her back to him and brushed it away from her face. "You won't have to," he promised. "It's over now. Try to believe that."

She shook her head desperately. "I feel if I lived to be a hundred I could never really feel it was over. It never *will* be over."

"It has to be," he said, "for Holly's sake. If you let her see you're still worried it'll darken her life."

She sighed. "Yes, I know you're right."

He drew her against him and she rested there, enjoying the comforting feel of his warmth. His arms were very strong around her, and it was a blessed relief to feel that here was someone who could take some of the burden from her shoulders. "We'd better be getting inside now," Jordan said, "or the little monkey will come chasing after us again."

They found Holly sitting at the computer, looking glumly at the blank screen. Jordan sat down and got to work, and within a few minutes he had everything working normally. "You see, it's not broken," he said. "You probably made so many demands on it all at once that you gave it a nervous breakdown."

Holly chuckled, happy again.

"One day," Jordan continued, "I'll show you how to hack into Cavendish Holdings. Though I'll probably regret it. I'll wake up and find I've sold off my most valuable assets for a song and bought a chain of ice-cream parlors."

"And it'll be your own fault," Veronica observed wryly. She was uneasy about the things Jordan was teaching Holly, but she didn't want to concern her daughter with her worries.

"I'm going to be a tycoon," Holly said gleefully. "I think tycooning is much more fun than playing Monopoly."

"Actually it's quite similar to Monopoly," Jordan remarked, "except that in real life the ramifications of what you do are far more serious than losing bits of paper or plastic."

"Teach me to be a tycoon," Holly begged.

"All right."

"Don't you think Holly's a bit young for that?" Veronica protested.

"She's not too young to learn the principles of success," Jordan said wickedly. He was happier than Veronica had ever seen him. Avoiding her critical eye, he proceeded to outline the basics. To Veronica's relief his description was simplified for Holly's childish ears, but even so it contained much that she disapproved of. Jordan's judgment had been swallowed up by his pride in the little girl, and she wondered if he guessed how much he looked like a doting father.

"Once you're interested in a property," he was saying, "you must study it carefully. Get to know its weak spots so that when the time comes you can acquire it on your own terms."

Holly nodded in solemn agreement with this obvious good sense.

"Always plan ahead," he went on. "Once you've set your heart on something, good intelligence work is vital. But play your cards close to your chest. It pays to keep the other side guessing and then take them by surprise."

"Like a dawn raid?" Holly demanded.

"That's right. A dawn raid means going around the stock brokers after the market has closed at night, buying up shares until you have a big stake in a company."

"Then its really an evening raid," Holly said, frowning.

"In a way, but the other side wakes up the next morning to find your foot in their door."

He went on to explain about shares in fairly simple language. Holly was entranced, hanging on Jordan's every word. He was an excellent teacher, Veronica realized, clear, concise and occasionally funny, illustrating his points vividly on the screen. Man and child were utterly absorbed and contented with each other.

She left them to it for an hour before saying, "Holly, I want you to go up for your nap now."

"Oh, Mommy—"

"Upstairs."

Reluctantly Holly stood up, looking at Jordan suspiciously. "Last time you went without saying goodbye to me," she accused.

"I won't do it again. Promise."

Mollified, she hugged him, then her mother, picked up the computer manual and departed quickly before she could be told to leave it behind. Jordan met Veronica's gaze sheepishly. "I know, I know," he said.

"May I ask what you think you're doing?" Veronica demanded. "I know she's bright, but I don't think she's ready for 'Tycooning in Six Easy Lessons,' or should it be 'How to Cut Throats and Influence People'? Save them until she's a bit older—say around her hundredth birthday."

"Come on, Ronnie. It's a game to her."

"It's a game to you, too. That's just the point. I don't want her to grow up into the sort of person to whom buying and selling people is fun."

"I don't buy and sell people."

"You buy and sell their livelihoods, and that's almost the same thing."

"Whose livelihood have I ever bought and sold?"

"Mine."

"If you mean Jezebel I thought I'd atoned for that."

"You have, but at the time all I knew was that my job had been snatched out from under me by someone who was using me as a pawn. It made me feel so helpless."

"What the hell...?" Jordan stopped as he realized he was raising his voice, and started again, "I don't know what you mean by 'pawn,' but whatever it is, that was a damned fool remark and I'm going away before you make another one and I lose whatever control I've managed to maintain."

He strode from the room. For an alarmed moment Veronica thought he was leaving altogether, but soon she heard him clattering in the kitchen, then going outside. When she went out a moment later she found him sprawled on a garden seat. It was the swinging kind with an awning overhead. He was absently levering the ground with his foot to maintain the motion, and drinking from a can of beer. When he saw her he slowed, patting the cushioned seat beside him, and she sat down. "Sourpuss," he chided her gently.

She sighed. "I know. I can't think what got into me."

"You're still upset from being alarmed about Holly. In fact, you're probably suffering a lingering depression from all the months you spent being frightened. That won't go suddenly just because she's all right now. It takes time."

"It takes forever. I'm beginning to realize that. I..." she hesitated.

"Go on," he said, taking her hand. "I think you need to talk about it."

"When Holly was so ill I felt I was staggering under a crushing weight, and I used to think that if only she could have the operation it would be lifted and I'd become happy and lighthearted at once. But I should have known better. It's only children who can shrug off the darkness because they don't know how easily it can return. Oh, Jordan, I still lie awake at night and go into her room to listen to her breathing. I get frightened all over again." Veronica smiled wryly. "She gets angry if she catches me."

He squeezed her hand. "That's natural. You can't expect children to understand how we love them. Holly's recovered from this a lot more quickly than you have, partly because she's young, but partly because she's had you to care for her. But who's looked after you?"

"At one time," she said slowly, "I'd have said I didn't need anyone to look after me. I was so proud of being able to manage alone, but...I don't know. I guess no one's that self-sufficient."

"No one should try to be if they don't have to," he told her gravely, and although his fingers were entwined with hers he seemed to be studying something in the distance.

Veronica's heart had begun to beat strongly as she understood what Jordan was really saying to her.

"No, I guess you're right," she said. "It's taken me a long time to learn that."

He didn't reply but lifted her hand to his mouth and lightly brushed his lips across the backs of her fingers. They sat in silence. All around them the summer day was at its height. The trees were quite still in the windless air, and the birds were quiet, as though too sleepy to sing.

"What became of Derek?" Jordan asked at last.

"We parted on good terms."

Something in Veronica's voice made him grin. "He must have done *something* to change your opinion of him."

"He told me that he didn't hold it against me that I'd had an illegitimate child."

"Damn him! What right did he have...? I hope you kicked him out bodily."

"I asked him to leave, but I didn't throw him out because in his way he's been kind to me. I know you think I'm making too much of this, but he *did* come to the hospital when Holly had her operation."

Jordan leaned back against the cushions and looked upward, shading his eyes against the light. "So did I."

She frowned at him, wondering if she'd misheard. "What did you say?"

He took down his arm and looked at her. "I was there too. I flew back from Paris to be with you, but I arrived too late. You were sitting in the hallway with Derek's arm around you."

She was torn between happiness and disappointment. "Jordan, why didn't you tell me?"

"There didn't seem much point. You didn't need me."

"Yes, I... You came all the way from Paris? Oh, heavens, all those things I said to you that day, about how kind Derek had been. Why did you let me make a fool of myself?"

"I couldn't get a word in edgewise," he protested. "You were in a fine temper."

"Besides, you find it hard to tell people what you've done for them, don't you?" she asked.

"What do you mean?"

"I mean this house. You rented it for us."

He shrugged. "Well, after I'd seen that dark little apartment of yours I had to do something. Holly needed the country. How did you find out?"

"Mrs. Hendricks told me, but I was bound to find out sooner or later. I was surprised as soon as I saw this place. It seemed so unlike you."

"Yes, my own apartment is purely functional. I'm not there very often anyway."

Veronica shuddered. "It doesn't sound like a home."

"It isn't. I have a place to sleep and a place to work—that's all I need."

"Is it? Is that really all you need, Jordan?"

He shook his head. "No. I need what you've had. You said you'd only been poor in money. I wonder if you know how blessed you look to me."

"I *do* know, because I look blessed to me, too."

"All those years I missed..." he said regretfully.

"I can show you, if you like," Veronica offered.

"How do you mean?"

"I've got some pictures of her as she was growing up. I brought them down here to start organizing them into albums, but I haven't finished."

"I'd love to see them." Jordan rose quickly and put out a hand for her. He almost ran across the lawn into the house.

Veronica led the way upstairs. "They're in here," she said, pushing open the door to her bedroom. Jordan sat on the bed while she rummaged in a drawer and finally brought out a photo album and a large brown paper envelope. Jordan opened the album at the first page, which showed one large picture of Veronica smiling down at the newborn baby she held in her arms. "My mother took that when Holly was four hours old," Veronica said.

Jordan didn't answer. He wasn't looking at Holly but at Veronica, her face radiant with joy and love.

He began to study the other pictures. There was Holly trying to walk, caught just at the moment when she'd sat down with a thump, her face full of indignation and surprise; Holly being held up by her grandmother to fix a bauble on the Christmas tree; Holly with her first tricycle; Holly building a house of cards, her face a mask of fierce concentration as she placed the top card; Holly and Veronica, their arms entwined, laughing into each other's face, enclosed by a golden circle of love. Jordan turned the pages in silence, looking at picture after picture, his face oddly expressionless to hide the pain within him.

Veronica, watching him for some sign of response, felt a pang of disappointment. His cold expression suggested that whatever he'd hoped to find in these pictures wasn't there. "I think I'll just look in on Holly for a moment," she said quietly.

"All right."

She rose quietly and gently pushed open the door to Holly's room. Holly lay on her stomach, one arm drooping over the side of the bed, the fingers just touching the computer manual that lay on the floor. She was sound asleep and breathing evenly. Veronica smiled and slipped away.

At the door to her own bedroom she stopped and her face softened. While she was away Jordan had stretched out on her bed, apparently to relax while he studied some loose pictures of Holly. But sleep must have overcome him almost immediately, and the pictures now lay on the counterpane where they'd fallen from his hand. His eyes were closed and his breathing came in a deep, regular rhythm that echoed Holly's.

Veronica closed the door and moved quietly to the bed to sit beside him. Now she could see the exhaustion that he'd hidden all day. There were dark smudges beneath his eyes, and his skin had the pallor of a man who spent too much time poring over papers, hurrying to and from airports and working through jet lag.

The sight brought back another time when she'd seen him pale and exhausted from long hours of study. His brilliant success had only carried him to another point on the treadmill, where there was still emptiness and the obsession to reach a goal that always retreated.

And it could have been so different, she realized. He might have looked much happier now if she'd shared Holly with him from the start.

Veronica suddenly grew very still. She was shocked to discover that she had instinctively used the word *shared*. It almost suggested that she'd behaved ungenerously in concealing his baby from him.

But I had no choice, she thought. *He didn't want either of us.*

But she quickly realized that she'd never given him the chance to say *what* he wanted.

He was the one who said we should stop seeing each other.

But he'd said it to Veronica, not to Holly.

The instantaneous attraction between Jordan and his daughter spoke for itself. It wasn't just his pride in her intelligence, it was the instinctive call of like to like, and it would have been there from the start. She knew now that he would have felt it the moment he held the sweet, soft, day-old bundle, and it would have opened his heart to a world of light and happiness that he'd never known before in his lonely life. She had banished him to his bleak inner desert, when she might have taken his hand and led him into the sunlight.

"How could I have done it?" she whispered softly.

She was filled with pain for the empty years, pain for his loss rather than her own. Hardly breathing, she reached up to touch his face. He stirred, moving so that his face was closer to her, and she laid her lips against his. At once she felt herself enfolded in his embrace. He held her tightly, pulling her onto the bed beside him, and began to run his hands over her. He spoke her name, but his eyes were still closed and she couldn't be sure how much of what he was doing he was aware of.

Jordan was in a place he knew well because he'd been there many times before, a half-sleeping, half-waking place, where it was dark and warm, and he could break out of the prison of unease and shyness that had walled him in all his life. The miserable sense that everyone else was speaking a language he didn't know left him, because here there was no language, only the instinctive communication of love. He didn't have to hold anything back. He could take his beloved into his arms and love her with his whole self, letting his lips and hands tell her what his inarticulate heart never could.

Her sweet young body was against his now. He had a temperature from the cold that had racked him for days, making his head stuffy and congested while he was taking his exams, but even through his fever he knew he was being burned by a fiercer flame. Veronica. His desire for her, so sternly suppressed before, had roared out of control at the touch of her naked flesh.

He dared to explore her, pulling her shirt out of the waistband of her jeans, tracing the tiny waist, then moving up to find the swell of her firm breasts. His hands encompassed them and the feel of the peaked nipples in his palms made him groan because it was even more tormentingly sweet than in his dreams.

Or perhaps he was dreaming now, as he'd dreamed so many times before. He felt hazy and didn't know if it was from the whiskey or the cold. But somewhere in the haze there was the fresh, warm scent of her body and the feel of her, solid and real for once, not fading away as always before. He opened his eyes and found Veronica in his arms.

For a moment he didn't know where he was. The sunny bedroom where he'd fallen asleep was less real than the shabby one-room apartment he'd lived in once, and where he'd dreamed he was again. Jordan began frantically to force his mind back, uncovering things he'd kept hidden for self-protection, knowing he was near the answer, and the chance might never come again.

On that night ten years ago he'd thought he'd held her naked body, touching her reverently and making her finally his own. But when he awoke he'd found her fully dressed and nowhere near the bed. Had it really happened, or was it only a fever-induced dream?

The thought of asking her outright had made him blush like the awkward boy he was. He began to edge clumsily toward what he desperately wanted to know.

"Good morning," he'd said.

She'd turned from where she was washing up. "Good morning."

Embarrassment had made him look away to ask, "Have you been here all night?"

"Yes."

The silence that followed had been cruel, swallowing all his hopes. When she'd spoken again it was to inquire briskly how he was. He'd forced himself to answer the same way, and then asked casually if she'd minded sleeping in the chair. She'd assured him she'd been quite comfortable and he'd known then that the beauty of their lovemaking had all been an illusion. The discovery had filled him with shame, as well as rejection.

For a long time afterward he couldn't think of that evening without going hot and cold, and soon he'd learned not to think of it at all. For ten years he'd rejected her as she'd rejected him.

But then she'd come back into his life, calling up memories he'd tried to forget. She said they'd made love and it was as if she'd looked into his heart that night and seen everything his pride had forced him to conceal. He'd reacted with raw sensitivity, refusing even to think that she might be telling the truth.

Now the illusion had come back, as bittersweet and tormenting as before, but this time, when he opened his eyes she was there, lying beside him, her shirt pulled open to the waist, her beautiful, satiny breasts cupped in his hands. "I thought I was dreaming," he murmured. "But you're here."

"I was the dream," she said softly.

"You were always the dream. But now..." He closed his eyes, more confused than he'd ever been in his life. What was real now could have been real then. If only he could disentangle past and present....

The ring of the telephone brought them both sharply back to reality. Jordan cursed and sat up. Veronica sighed. Never had a call been so ill-timed. She answered, and after a moment handed the receiver to Jordan. "It's Kate," she said.

He took the receiver, frowning with annoyance. He listened briefly before saying, "Thanks for calling me, Kate." He hung up and said, "I have to make another call."

"I'll leave you, then." She left the room, and as she went downstairs she could hear him dialing.

She was dazed at what had happened. For a moment she'd looked into Jordan's eyes and what she'd seen was startled understanding. She could see that illusion and reality had mingled for him, but she couldn't tell if he'd accepted all the implications.

She would never know now what might have happened between them if the phone hadn't rung. Even if he stayed, the moment had passed. But she had a feeling he wasn't going to.

A moment later he came downstairs. "I'm afraid I've got to go," he said regretfully. "I thought the deal was all sewn up but..." He shrugged.

"Never mind," she said, trying not to let her disappointment overcome her.

"I promised Holly I wouldn't go without saying goodbye. May I wake her up?"

Veronica nodded and followed him upstairs. Holly was still lying on her stomach. Veronica watched from the doorway as Jordan sat on the bed and tickled her cheek gently with a finger. "Wake up," he whispered. Holly opened her eyes at once, rolling over on her back and smiling when she saw who it was. "I have to go, pet."

"Oh, no, *please* don't."

"I must. But we'll see more of each other in the future, I promise. Trust me."

"Tell me about it," Holly pleaded.

"Not just yet. I've got plans but...not just yet." He hugged Holly.

Veronica went downstairs as he followed a few minutes later. "What did you mean just then?" she asked.

He looked oddly uncomfortable. "This isn't the moment. I hate going away now, but I don't have any choice. Damn, why did this have to happen now just as we...that is, I... There's so much we have to talk about."

"Yes," she said expectantly, "so very much."

He seemed about to say something else, but instead he pulled her into his arms and said everything that way. The sense of incredible delight that he could bring her swept through her again, and she felt herself melting. She kissed him back, letting the urgent movements of her lips tell him that she loved him and never wanted to let him go. Tremors went through him as he divined her silent message through all his senses. "Ronnie," he said hoarsely, "Ronnie...*I must go....*"

"Yes, you must," she murmured.

"Let me go," he pleaded desperately.

Her arms were around him but only lightly, in an embrace he could have broken in a moment. "I'm not stopping you," she whispered against his mouth.

"That's not true and you know it," he grated.

Veronica dropped her arms but left her lips against his. "Go away," she said.

With a mighty effort Jordan put his hands on her shoulders and stepped back. "Heaven help me, I don't know whether I'm coming or going," he said. "Don't come outside or I'll never force myself away."

He went to the door and left like a man escaping danger. A few seconds later Veronica heard his car going down the driveway.

She stayed where she was, dazed with a happiness. It wasn't only the passion she'd felt in his touch and heard in his voice. Today Jordan had called her Ronnie. Since he'd discovered her deception on the night of their reunion she'd been "Veronica," a person he distrusted. But he could open his heart to Ronnie, and he'd revealed his true feelings in ways he probably didn't suspect.

She went upstairs and began to put away the photographs, studying each one, trying to see how it must have looked to him. Happiness was giving way to an aching sense of frustration. They'd come so close to understanding each other, and then it had all been snatched away.

The phone rang and she answered it hopefully. It might be Jordan to say he was coming back....

"Hello," said the woman on the other end. "I want to speak to Jordan."

Veronica stiffened. She knew that sugary voice and felt threatened by its owner. "I'm afraid he's already left," she said.

There was a fractional pause before Lorrayne said, "How long ago?"

"Half an hour."

"Oh, then I'd better hurry. It looks like he'll be early for our date and he hates to be kept waiting. Poor darling, I'm not very punctual and I'm afraid I drive him quite mad."

"I understood he'd returned to London to work," Veronica said coldly.

Lorrayne responded with a rich chuckle. "Oh, no, did he say that? What a lark! On second thought, though, it's not funny. He assured me that he'd talked to you and that you understood. It seems he hasn't. It's really very naughty of him."

"Understood?" Veronica whispered.

"Well, darling, if I'm prepared to be understanding about you, it seems only fair for you to be understanding about me."

"And you're prepared to be 'understanding' about me?" Veronica demanded.

"For a while—yes. You see, I do appreciate that you're in a difficult position, and naturally I'm prepared to make allowances."

"That's extremely kind of you," Veronica said ironically. "May I just ask what you're prepared to make allowances about?"

"Well, really, I think that's rather a silly question. It hasn't been easy for me to adjust to the situation, but we all know whose interests have to come first, don't we? How is Holly, by the way? I thought she was such a sweet child."

Shivers of alarm went up Veronica's spine. "Please leave my daughter out of this, Miss Haslam."

"It's Mrs., actually."

Veronica's growing rage put an edge on her tongue. "Oh, yes, you specialize in husbands, don't you? Rich ones, usually."

"Rich ones always, darling. Give me credit for using my intelligence."

"I doubt if your intelligence had anything to do with it," Veronica snapped.

Lorrayne chuckled again. "On the contrary, intelligence comes into it a good deal. It takes far more than alluring looks, which is why I'm where I am, and you're where you are. You played your cards cleverly up to a point, I'll grant you, but you lacked the final *je ne sais quoi* to land a really big fish."

"Considering how long you've been trying to land this fish, I'd say your *je ne sais quoi* has been running low recently," Veronica retorted with spirit. "I'm not going to bandy words with you, Mrs. Haslam—"

"No, it is getting boring, isn't it? Give my love to Holly."

Lorrayne hung up.

Slowly Veronica replaced the receiver, feeling the chill invade her heart, colder, colder, until she was like ice.

What a fool she'd been! What a gullible, willing, easily deceived fool! This woman knew the truth. Jordan must have discussed her and Holly with Lorrayne. He'd said, or at least hinted, that Holly was his daughter. He hadn't admitted it to Holly's mother, but he had to Lorrayne, because Lorrayne figured in his future plans and Veronica didn't.

His words to Holly earlier that day had certainly been prophetic. *"Acquire a property on your own terms...plan ahead...play your cards close to your chest...keep the other side guessing."*

Had he realized how he was giving himself away? No, because he thought Veronica would never see through the cloud of deceit and pretended love he was spinning around her. Nor *would* she have seen through it, but for the lucky chance of Lorrayne's call.

She'd known about Lorrayne, yet foolishly she'd let him entrance her until she'd forgotten the troublesome questions. And all the time he'd been playing his cards close to his chest, deluding her until she would hand over the paper in which he denied paternity, without which he couldn't acquire Holly on his own terms.

The bright mirage of love that she'd built up had dissolved before her eyes, revealing a man who was false in everything.

The ice in her heart was thawing now, giving way to a hard, terrible pain. She braced herself against it, fighting back the unshed tears. She had no time to cry. Only action would help her, and it must be speedy.

Chapter Ten

The day after Lorrayne's call Veronica moved Holly and herself back to London. Holly was surprised by the sudden decision, but she didn't question it as vigorously as Veronica had feared. She seemed preoccupied, spending almost all her time reading or playing with the computer. Normally Veronica would have noticed how strangely quiet she was and asked anxious questions, but now the urgent need to get out of Jordan's house swept everything else from her mind.

As soon as they reached home she called Sally to say she was available for work. Sally greeted her with delight and promised to be in touch soon.

Holly's spirits rose as the day for her final checkup neared. She was lively during the journey and when they arrived at the doctor's office she hopped out and bounded up to the front door. Dr. Weston laughed when he saw her and said, "I don't really need to ask, do I? Come on, let's have a look at that scar."

Holly pulled off her T-shirt and displayed the big scar on her chest. The sight still horrified Veronica, but Holly was tremendously proud of it. She stood at attention while the doctor examined the places where the stitches had been, and when he got out his stethoscope she immediately went into the breathing routine she knew he wanted.

He listened to her heart and grunted with satisfaction. "Steady as a bass drum," he declared, putting the stethoscope away. "Everything's healed beautifully." He extended his hand to Holly. "It's been a pleasure knowing you, Miss Grant," he said solemnly, "but we won't be seeing each other again."

Holly giggled and shook his hand. The doctor smiled at Veronica and said, "Try not to be overprotective. She's as fit as any other child of her age now."

In her heart Veronica had known that, but she felt an incredible relief at hearing the words. "I don't know how to thank you adequately," she told the doctor.

He waved thanks aside and ushered them out. "Can I have one last ride on Toby?" Holly pleaded when they were in the corridor. Toby was a large wooden horse that stood in the entrance and was set in motion by a coin in a slot. Holly climbed onto his back, seized the reins and cried "Giddyup" as he began to heave. Veronica watched her, smiling with pleasure.

Then her smile faded as she looked past Holly to the man who'd just entered the lobby. Jordan stood there looking at her, his expression filled with accusation, while Toby reared and plunged between them, and Holly drove him on with excited cries.

This was the first time she'd seen or spoken to Jordan since he'd held her in his arms at Elmbridge, whispering words of passion and longing that had thrilled her. But the discovery of how he'd deceived her had caused her heart to harden against him, and now she faced him as a hostile stranger. To the pain of disillusioned love was added an overwhelming fear. Jordan was an acquisitive man. When Veronica thought of Lorrayne Haslam waiting in the wings, her fighting spirit rose.

As Toby came to a halt Holly spotted Jordan and held out her arms to be helped down. At once the anger went out of his face and he reached for her, smiling.

"I'm better," she announced. "The doctor says I'm like a bass drum, and we won't be seeing each other again, and Mommy isn't to be overprotective, but I guess she will, anyway." Lack of breath brought her to a halt.

"That's wonderful," Jordan said, laughing. "How about going to my office for a celebration?" He added conspiratorially, "I've got some computers there that'll make your eyes pop."

"Yes, please," she said, slipping her hand into his.

Veronica had no choice but to smile and agree.

In the car Holly chattered happily, covering the uneasy silence between the other two. She was fascinated when Jordan pointed out to her the great glass-and-concrete building that was the headquarters of Cavendish Holdings, and stared determinedly out of the window to catch every detail as they swept into the underground car park.

Once in the elevator, Jordan pointed to a button for Holly to press, and they were taken directly up to his office. It was a large corner room with plate glass on two sides. Holly made her way along both sides, looking down into the street five floors below and across to the windows of other buildings. Her face bore a look of wonder, such as most children would have felt on a trip to Disneyland.

Holly had reached the windows that faced the huge billboard that had once displayed her mother's picture. Jordan glanced at Veronica with raised eyebrows, and she knew he was reminding her that her daughter might have seen that picture.

He believes I'm a bad mother, she thought angrily. But what right does he have to judge me? Beneath her anger there was alarm as she remembered how he'd once said Holly needed "careful handling" with an implied claim that he could do better than Veronica.

Jordan called Kate Adams in and introduced Holly. "I'd like you to take Holly on the grand tour," he told her. When they'd departed he turned to Veronica, his eyes hard with anger. "I called you this morning and Mrs. Hendricks informed me you'd left Elmbridge several days ago. You didn't even tell me you were leaving. I wouldn't have known you were here if she hadn't said it was the day for Holly's final checkup. *My own daughter*, and you kept me in the dark."

Veronica drew in her breath sharply. "Since when have you called Holly your daughter?" she demanded.

"Does it matter?" he asked impatiently. "Of course she's my daughter. That's obvious."

She'd dreamed of this moment, but now it was here she felt only a knot of fear in her stomach. There was no tenderness in Jordan's manner as he discussed his child with that child's mother. He was brisk and efficient, as he would have been with anything he'd decided to take over.

"It wasn't always so obvious to you," she reminded him.

"Are you holding that against me? I understand things now that I didn't then. You sprang her on me out of the blue. I was bound to be suspicious."

"You've always said she couldn't be yours because you didn't remember making love. Are you saying you've remembered?"

He hesitated. "I'm not sure. But I've come to see how it could be true."

"You mean you've decided to accept it because it now suits you to do so," she said with a shrewdness that made Jordan wince.

He regarded Veronica in baffled annoyance, irked that she should choose to make a simple matter complicated. He wasn't used to having his decisions questioned, except by his enemies, but he could deal with them. His employees knew better than to argue and Lorrayne had always fallen in with his wishes for practical reasons. Even when he'd recently brought their association to an end, she'd been reasonable: suspiciously reasonable, he might have thought, if he had paused to consider. But he'd ascribed her yielding to the magnificent diamond necklace he'd given her as a parting present.

Now Veronica was not only disputing his decision but challenging him to explain himself, and nothing in his previous experience had taught him how to cope with such a situation. As he felt the ground shift beneath him his manner grew more brusque. "Let's not get melodramatic. You told me Holly was my daughter, and now I accept that she is. What more can there be to say?"

"From one point of view, nothing," she said, looking at him curiously.

"Then let's view the situation practically. It's Holly's future that matters."

"You've already taken care of her future very well, just by giving her one," Veronica said.

Jordan searched her face but could find none of the pleasure he'd looked forward to seeing. To cover his aching dismay he began to talk quickly, hoping something would banish her unyielding look that hurt like a door slammed in his face. "The question is what kind of life she's going to have. I've been thinking where she should go to school, and there's a place called Briars, where they take only very gifted pupils. It would stretch her intelligence and she'd be happy there. The headmaster thinks she sounds ideal and—"

"Just a moment," she interrupted him. "Do you mean you've discussed Holly with the headmaster without first speaking to me? How *dare* you! Do I have to remind you that I'm her mother and legal guardian?"

"It seems that *I* have to remind *you* that I'm her father. She's an exceptional child and I mean to see that she's given the chance to fulfill her potential."

"*You* mean to see...? That's my job."

"Have you been doing it? Has she been getting the education she needs?"

"Of course she hasn't. She's been ill."

"She's also been taught by incompetent teachers who prefer children as mediocre as themselves. I'm not blaming you. Special schools cost money, which you haven't got. But I can give her what she needs and it only made sense to start making arrangements."

"Sense to you, possibly, but I'll make any arrangements necessary. We left Elmbridge because from now on, Holly and I won't be troubling you any longer."

"What the devil do you mean?"

"I mean this is the last time we'll have any contact. You've kept your side of the bargain to the letter and I thank you. Now I'm keeping mine. There'll be no claims on you, nothing. As far as you're concerned, Holly and I no longer exist."

He heard her words blankly. Their meaning was so monstrous that his brain seemed to scramble them, protecting him from understanding. "What are you saying?" he asked stupidly.

"I'm saying goodbye. I won't give Holly up to you, Jordan. She still needs me. This is one takeover you can't force through."

He shook his head, trying to clear it. "Have I asked you to give her up?"

"You've made it plain you want to replace me as her guardian—"

"Look, wait a minute." He held up a hand. "There's been a misunderstanding. My idea is for us to get married, but I should have made that clear at the start."

Veronica regarded him in astonishment. A proposal of marriage was the last thing she'd expected to hear, and for a brief moment her heart leaped. Then the dimensions of Jordan's real plan burst on her and she gave a hard laugh. "Thank you for informing me of 'your idea,'" she said. "That has to be the most earthshaking proposal of marriage any woman ever received."

Something deep inside him flinched at her irony. It wasn't how he'd meant to do it, but he hadn't anticipated that she would shut him out of Holly's big day, either. Nor could he have foreseen having to propose through a haze of hurt feelings to a coolly angry woman who saw all his good intentions in the least flattering light.

He thought of how happy this moment might have been, and disappointment made him cruel. "What did you expect?" he demanded sarcastically. "Moonlight and roses? A little inappropriate in our circumstances, don't you think?"

"Totally," she snapped. "Especially considering that what you're really doing is setting up a deal. You're not a father, you're a corporate raider. Am I supposed to be overwhelmed with gratitude because you've finally decided to accept Holly? Well, I'm not, because I've seen how carefully you looked her over first to see if she was up to standard. You didn't want her until you knew she was a child to be proud of. You've been studying the property and now you think it's worth acquiring, even if you have to take me with it. Of course, you wouldn't have to keep me for long, just long enough to stake your legal claim to Holly, and then divorce me and keep her. It's known as asset stripping, and I've heard you're very good at it."

Jordan went paler than she'd ever seen anyone go before. He looked as if he was struggling against a fatal wound. "You're a pretty good fighter yourself, Veronica. You know how to identify a man's weak spot and plunge the knife right in. So I don't have to be too particular about the weapons I use to fight you back, do I?

"You could have had it the easy way—kept Holly, and had anything you wanted in the bargain. But if you prefer to play dirty, we will, and you have yet to discover just how dirty I can play. Once the court sees those Jezebel pictures they'll wonder if you're fit to be a mother."

"They'll also wonder why you're so concerned about a child who isn't yours," she flung back at him. "I have it in black and white, Jordan, signed, sealed and witnessed. *Holly is not your daughter.* Once I hated you for making me sign that, but now I'm glad because any action you bring against me to claim Holly will collapse the moment I produce it."

It was true. In his bitter rage he'd forgotten about the weapon that he himself had put into her hands. She could deny him his child and he could do nothing about it. Aghast, Jordan stared at the desert he'd created by his own actions, and at himself, stranded in it.

"You'd really do it, wouldn't you?" he said raggedly. "You'd take Holly away and never let me see her again."

"You leave me no choice. If I gave you half a chance you'd take her over, lock, stock and barrel, but I'll stop you because I don't want her to grow up thinking nothing matters but the next deal or the next share issue, or manipulating people the way you've tried to manipulate me."

"The way I've...?"

"I don't trust you, Jordan. Holly's a sweet child with a lovely nature, but there's enough of you in her to make her detached and calculating if she's taught the wrong things. I know you can make her a great heiress, but I also know the price she'd end up paying. I don't want to see her grow up cold and loveless, like you."

Jordan's expression was murderous. "It's easy to talk like that when you've had everything, isn't it?" he raged. "Cold and loveless, yes, but I didn't have to be. I had a child that I would have loved from the start if I'd been allowed to know her, a child who might have loved me back.

"Do you know what it did to me when you showed me a picture of you holding Holly when she was four hours old and told me your mother had taken it? Damn you, *I* should have taken it. I should have helped her walk and mended her toys and held her up to decorate the Christmas tree—but I wasn't given the chance, was I?

"My parents were both dead before I was two and I had no other relatives. Holly is the only person in the world who's *my own flesh and blood*. You couldn't understand that because you've always had a family, but she's the only family I've ever had and you took her away from me. You kept her for yourself like a miser hoarding treasure, and now you dare to blame me because I'm poor."

The silence was dreadful. Veronica stared at Jordan, her face ravaged by his accusations. In a few shattering moments he'd laid bare the desolate wastes of his life, wastes for which he blamed her. She closed her eyes against the pictures he'd conjured up, but they were still there, pictures of a heart grown withered for lack of use. And it was all needless, because there was a little girl who could have made the desert flower, but he hadn't known her until it was too late.

He, too, stood in stunned silence, as though by putting the cruel truth into words he'd forced himself to see it clearly for the first time.

Before either of them could speak the door opened and Holly bounced in, eager to tell everything she'd seen. But she stopped when she saw them standing there, motionless, and felt the air jagged between them. Her eyes went to her mother's face and the misery she saw there made her run to Veronica crying, "Mommy!"

"It's all right, pet." Veronica hastily recovered herself.

But Holly wasn't fooled. She reached up to pull her mother down to a nearby chair where she could see her better. She seemed to look past Veronica's bright smile and forced cheerfulness to something that couldn't be hidden.

Then she slipped her arms around her mother's neck and moved closer to her in a gesture that was oddly protective. Her eyes, on Jordan, were filled with silent accusation. He understood her message without words and looked away. Veronica clenched her hands, and despite everything her heart ached for Jordan. What Holly had just done had broken his heart. "I think the two of you should leave now," he said with a trace of huskiness in his voice.

She rose with Holly's hand in hers and started going through the polite formalities, still hoping the worst could be hidden from Holly. "Thank you for letting Holly see around your building," she said. "You really enjoyed it, didn't you, Holly?"

"Very much, thank you," Holly said mechanically, her eyes on Jordan.

Veronica drew her to the door. Jordan made no move to follow them.

We'll never see each other again, she thought. How can it all end like this?

But it was going to. She said goodbye in polite, meaningless words that covered her heartbreak. Holly hardly spoke, but she paused a moment in the doorway for a last look at him. Jordan was turned their way but Veronica couldn't tell which of them he was looking at. His face was a frozen mask that expressed nothing at all.

Chapter Eleven

It wasn't hard to track down The Briars, the school Jordan had mentioned. Veronica took Holly to see it and a talk with the headmaster soon convinced her that Holly would be happy there, with her intelligence stretched to its limit. Holly seemed to think so, too, because she looked eagerly at everything and asked a lot of questions.

Veronica paled a little when she saw the fee schedule, but she put Holly's name down for the next term. She would manage somehow because Holly must have the chance she was entitled to. Despite her heartache Veronica was grateful to Jordan for showing her something she hadn't realized herself.

Sally called a few days later. "Rick was delighted to hear you're back in the land of the living and he wants you to work for him," she said.

"I don't want to be nude again," Veronica said quickly. Rick was the photographer who'd taken the Jezebel pictures.

"Nothing like that. It's designer jeans."

"That sounds harmless."

Sally set up the session, and Veronica went along to Rick's studio. He greeted her with a hug, and she punched him playfully. They'd worked together several times and got along well. He was a skinny young man who wore his hair cropped close, and cultivated a hard, intimidating expression. But beneath it he was absurdly soft-hearted, and his favorite topic of conversation was his pregnant wife. Over a cup of coffee he and Veronica swapped baby lore, until he suddenly said, "You've changed."

"How?" she demanded, alarmed lest she'd become unemployable.

"Your face is thinner...but it's not just that. There's something new there. Stay where you are." He turned a camera on her and studied her through the lens. "I can see it better like this," he announced. "Smile." She did so, and he nodded. "You haven't been smiling enough."

With the aid of his camera Rick had an almost uncanny talent for analyzing people and faces. The lens wasn't deceived by her cheerful front. It saw through it to the sadness that pervaded her inwardly.

He took a Polaroid snapshot and showed it to her. At once she could see the change in her own face, not just thinner, but the haunted look of a woman who'd bidden farewell to the joys of life for the second time, and knew that this time was final.

"I'll have to do this a different way," he mused. "No smiles. Look pensive."

"In jeans?"

"Yes, great. It's what people don't expect."

She began to make up to his directions. Then she brushed the glorious mass of her hair until it gleamed copper and gold in the brilliant lights. "Beautiful," Rick commented, studying her through the lens again. "The camera really loves you, Ronnie. Those Jezebel pix were the best thing I ever did. When I think that it all went to waste..." He groaned at the memory.

"You'll be careful what happens to the unused ones, won't you?" she said. "I'd hate to think there were nude pictures of me floating around."

He lowered the camera to stare at her in surprise. "I don't have any unused ones. Jordan Cavendish took the whole lot."

"He *what*?"

"Didn't you know? It's not something I'll forget in a hurry. It was straight after I heard the news the ads were canceled because he'd taken over. He came around here one day and said that Cavendish Holdings owned the copyright to every last one of those pictures and he wanted them—prints, negatives, everything.

"I refused at first, but not for long. He had a wild look in his eyes that meant trouble, and as I'm a Grade A coward I caved in. He went through them and kept saying, 'Are you sure there aren't any more?' I didn't know how to convince him. But by then I'd figured out that this was personal—"

"What do you mean?"

"Come on, Ronnie. If it was just business he could have sent someone else to collect them. This man's time is money. According to one paper he makes a thousand pounds a minute, so allowing time for traveling it must have cost him nearly a hundred thousand to come here. Of course it was personal.

"Besides, I saw his face. Those pictures really got to him. He'd have liked to have killed me for seeing you naked." Rick became a little embarrassed. "When you vanished from circulation I thought—well, let's say I'm surprised to see you working again."

"I vanished from circulation because my daughter had major surgery and needed me," Veronica informed him crisply.

"Yes, but—Look, Ronnie, don't pretend to be dim. If a bloke with that kind of money is all worked up about you I'd say your troubles were over. Know what I mean?"

"I know exactly what you mean and you couldn't be more wrong," Veronica said with a glint in her eyes that warned him to go no further. "Mr. Cavendish is an old acquaintance who very kindly took an interest in what he felt to be an undesirable development in my career. There is nothing between us."

Rick gulped. "As bad as that?" he asked. "All right, 'nuff said. Let's get to work."

Veronica got into position and began following his instructions automatically. Beneath her calm, professional surface she was in turmoil at what she'd just learned.

She'd taken it for granted that Jordan had vetoed her as Jezebel out of revenge for her setting him up—as he'd thought. But what Rick had just told her didn't sound like cold-blooded revenge.

Phrases reverberated through her mind... *"A wild look in his eye...he'd have liked to have killed me for seeing you naked..."* The words reminded her of something else she'd heard recently, but she couldn't quite place the echo.

Then it came to her with such a shock that she sat up sharply, causing a yelp of protest from behind the lens.

It had been Jordan. *"A man who loved you would have been torn apart by those pictures. He'd have sold his house, gone in rags, mortgaged his very soul, anything to stop other men seeing what belonged to him."*

A man who loved you...

Jordan had never told her he loved her, but he was a man who would find it difficult to say. He'd shown her in a thousand ways what she meant to him, and she'd been blind. But perhaps she'd been blind all along.

Her body turned this way and that but her mind had slipped away to another time when everything had meant twice as much, because she was seventeen and in love. It was a special time, when the man she loved was wonderful not only for himself but because he was taking her into worlds she'd never dreamed of before. The colors were brighter and the wine sweeter, the joy more dazzling and the pain more shattering than they would ever be again.

One evening they'd sat in her cramped little apartment sharing a hamburger, and he'd said, "My final exams are coming up. I've got to concentrate. Perhaps we'd better not see each other for a while."

And she'd smiled and responded, "Sure. I'm going to be a bit busy myself."

"That's all right then." She thought he would leave right away under the circumstances, but he sat there, looking awkward. "You're sure you don't mind?" he asked at last.

"Of course I don't mind, silly. Do you think I can't live if I don't see you every day?" She dug him playfully in the ribs. "You've got quite a swelled head, haven't you?"

He got to his feet. "Right then, I'll be going."

"Fine. Give me a call sometime."

"Sure."

"Just to let me know how the exams are going."

"Right."

"Only if you have a moment," she said desperately. "It's not important."

"Fine."

"Fine."

She knew he wouldn't call her. He was putting her out of his life so that she couldn't distract him from his goal. In that moment she hated him, but she'd covered it with a bright smile that stayed frozen on her face until the door had closed behind him. Then it faded slowly while she stared into space, the expression in her eyes as blank as the future.

She'd sat quite still, almost fearing to breathe lest she miss the sound of him going downstairs, the front door opening and closing, then his footsteps in the street. The sounds had stopped suddenly and there was a long silence. She'd wanted to go to the window and feast her eyes on him one last time, but she hadn't. She was bitterly hurt and angry and too proud to look out because she knew if she did she would watch him until he disappeared around the corner, and he might guess that she loved him when he cared so little for her. So she stayed motionless, gripping the arms of the chair, until the sound of footsteps started again, fading into the distance until she could hear them no more.

Pride could be a good thing. She'd kept her pride that night and was glad of it. Yet what haunted her now, like a reproach, was the memory of the silence before he'd walked away, as though he was standing beneath her window, looking up, not too proud to let her know he longed for a last sight of her.

It was too late now. She would never know what might have happened. But she knew that if she had it to do over again she would go to the window.

Days had turned into weeks. He hadn't called and she had forced herself not even to think of calling him, lest she weaken. Winter dragged on and the cold weather lasted into April. The ground was as hard as stone, as hard as the pain in her heart.

One evening her landlady knocked on the door, calling "Phone!" and Veronica hurried downstairs to the hall where the communal telephone was kept.

It was Jordan. When her heart had calmed its violent beating she realized that he sounded terrible. His voice was hoarse and scratchy and he could barely speak above a whisper. "I just called to say hello," he told her, trying to sound cheerful.

"Jordan, whatever's the matter with you?"

"Nothing's the matter with me."

"You sound awful."

"Just a little cold."

"Are you calling from home?" "Home" in Jordan's case meant a shabby boarding house where he rented a room and, like her, shared a communal phone.

"Yes, why?" he asked.

"Because you're standing down in that freezing hallway when you should be in your warm room," she said worriedly.

He tried to laugh and went off into a spasm of coughing. When he'd recovered he said, "That's all the thanks I get for calling you. Never mind me. How are you getting on?"

"I'm fine," she said mechanically.

"That's great. I'm fine, too."

"I've got a new part."

"Great."

"How are you managing in your exams?"

There was a long silence and she wondered if he'd heard her. "Jordan?"

"I'm here." After hesitating some more he said slowly, "I'm making a mess of the exams, Ronnie."

"But why? You're so brilliant."

"No one can be brilliant feeling as I do," he confessed.

"Have you got many more exams?"

"Two—the big ones. The first one's tomorrow."

She crossed her fingers. "What you need is a friend to come and look after you," she said tentatively.

Another silence, while she could hear her heart beating. "I guess I do," he said hoarsely.

"I'll be right over. Get back into your bed."

Her heart was light as she hurried out. He'd called because he wanted to see her, hoping she would offer to come. She was going to be with him again, and for a moment that was all that mattered.

There was a small supermarket on her way where she could buy milk and some whiskey. Her cash stock was low but she still had a little in the bank. She found the cash machine and, praying hard, pushed her plastic card in. The machine informed her that she had only five pounds left, which would be enough for a half bottle of whiskey. She took the money and hurried to the shop.

She reached the boarding house half an hour later and ran up the stairs to his room. He opened the door in his robe and pajamas. He was coughing and seemed feverish. The room was a mess. His bed looked as if he'd been tossing in it and his books, which he usually kept in perfect order, were scattered higgledy-piggledy.

"It's all right—Florence Nightingale has arrived," she said briskly, to hide the fact that her heart was thumping at the sight of him. She ordered him out of the draft and poured some milk into a pan on his hot plate while he sat on the bed, watching her and looking dejected. "Thanks, Ronnie," he said in a muffled voice.

"Don't mention it. What are friends for?"

His eyes widened when she produced the whiskey. "Where did you get that?"

"I robbed a liquor store, of course. How else would I get whiskey?"

"On your wages I can believe it. Ronnie, you're wonderful."

"It's a miracle cure." She was mixing a concoction of half warm milk, half whiskey with a liberal helping of sugar. "Drink it up."

While he drank she stripped his bed and remade it from scratch. When it was finished it looked neat and inviting, and Jordan climbed in thankfully. Then she took his empty mug and got to work, and a few minutes later she was back at the bedside with another drink. She sat on the bed while he drank and glanced at the book he'd taken with him. "Can't you rest?" she asked.

"I can't stop," he whispered. "I'm doing so badly with this cold. I can't think. I sit in that exam room and I can feel my chances slipping away."

"You can take the exams again."

"No," he said frantically. "I've got to get ahead quickly.... There's no time. Look at this room. I don't want to go on living in places like this.... It's got to be now...." He started coughing.

She left him, knowing there was no way she could reach him through the haze of his obsession. But when she'd washed up she turned back and found him asleep, the book slipping from his hand.

She crept quietly around the room gathering up his dirty laundry, took his key and slipped out to the launderette on the next road. She was back in an hour with everything washed and dried, to find him just beginning to stir. Without putting on the light she sat on the bed and felt his forehead. It seemed cooler, and she realized thankfully that her treatment was working.

"Ronnie..." he whispered.

"I'm here." She leaned farther over him, and he put up his hands to touch her. His eyes were still closed.

"Why are you wearing all that stuff?" he asked as he encountered her duffle coat.

"I've been out," she explained, stripping the coat off.

He didn't seem to hear, but went on muttering, "Always hiding from me.... You drive me mad." He reached up again and discovered that the coat was gone. He began to move his fingers over her shirt until he found her neck, slipped a hand around it and drew her down to him. Veronica held him close, his face against her breasts, feeling the misery of the past few weeks drain away.

He seemed to be asleep again and lay for a long time without moving. Veronica hardly dared breathe for fear he would awaken and turn away. Her arms had ached to hold him, and the feel of him was inexpressibly sweet to her. Moving gently, she began to stroke his tousled hair. He stirred and took hold of her hand, drawing it down his cheek and turning his head to kiss it. His breath burned her, and the touch of his lips in her palm sent tremors of delight along her arm.

His tongue began to flicker softly against her skin and she drew a long, ragged breath, fighting to stay still. Jordan had never done that before, and it was sending new sensations through her. They'd shared kisses in the past, knowing the risk but guarding against it, or so they'd assured themselves. But this was different. This wasn't the onslaught of straightforward desire to be fought head-on. This was a subtle, tantalizing eroticism that had slid past her defenses before she realized the danger.

"Ronnie..." he whispered.

"Yes, my love...my darling." She held her breath when she'd said this because she'd never come so near to revealing her deepest feelings before. The room was almost in darkness, the only light coming from the one-bar electric fire. She could feel him, warm and trembling in her arms, but she could barely see him. A slight gleam told her that his eyes had opened, but she couldn't make out their expression.

"Ronnie...?" he said again, faintly questioning as if not sure he'd heard right.

"My dearest love." Then her feelings overwhelmed her and she drew him close, murmuring, "Jordan, I love you so much."

He began to caress her with increasing urgency. She helped him by pulling off her clothes, eager to feel his touch. She knew she was mad and there could be no future for them, but tonight love was stronger than caution. Just this once she would claim him and live on the memory all her life if she had to.

So she held him close and welcomed him. In her heart she'd been his for a long time. Now she was his in fact. And belonging to him was as overwhelming and as beautiful as she'd dreamed it would be. Afterward she lay for hours, listening to his steady breathing, clasping him in loving possessiveness. And she knew that whatever happened, as long as she lived, she would never regret what she had done. Better a thousand misfortunes than to live and die without ever having been one with her beloved.

He slept without moving, his head pillowed on her breast, all restlessness gone from him. As the first light began to appear between the cracks of the curtains she pushed him gently away and eased herself silently out of the bed. She didn't want to let him find her naked in his arms. Last night had been another world when they'd claimed each other in the darkness, unashamed. Today, in the cold, ugly light of morning, she was strangely shy.

He awoke to find her fully dressed, filling the kettle. "Good morning," he said uncertainly.

She turned and looked at him out of shining eyes.

"Good morning."

"What time is it?"

"Eight o'clock."

He regarded her, frowning, then abruptly looked away. "Have you been here all night?" he asked.

Her smile faded. "Yes," she said, and waited. But he didn't answer and the silence went on and on. "How are you feeling now?" she asked at last.

"Fine, much better. I think I'll get through all right now, thanks to you."

"Good. I'm glad."

He laughed awkwardly. "Poor Ronnie. I never meant to put you to so much trouble. Was it very uncomfortable, sleeping in the chair? Or did you have to make do with the floor?"

Pain spread through her. For her their lovemaking had been wonderful, momentous. For him it hadn't even happened. Briefly she considered telling him, but rejected the idea at once. The thought of trying to convey her sense of joy to a man who would only stare at her blankly appalled her.

Besides, the beauty came from what they'd shared, the closeness and intimacy she'd felt in his arms, held against his heart. Now she learned there'd been no sharing. By not remembering, Jordan had destroyed it for her. "I slept on the chair, and it was quite comfortable," she assured him.

"I didn't disturb you, making noise or tossing about."

"You never moved," she said quietly.

He got out of bed and picked up the empty whiskey bottle. "You can't afford this," he said, scandalized when he saw the price, which she'd forgotten to remove.

"Actually I'm quite flush at the moment," she lied, turning back to the washing up.

"Still, I must repay you—when I can. In the meantime I'll give you an I.O.U."

"There's no need," she said shortly.

"I like to pay my debts."

"I said there's no need!" she shouted. After a glance at his shocked expression she dried her hands quickly. "It's about time I was going."

"Why are you angry with me?"

"I'm not angry with you, but you're all right now."

"Have I done something?"

"No. Leave me alone. I've got to go."

"Thanks for all you've done for me, Ronnie."

"That's all right. Good luck with the exam."

She'd left as quickly as she could and run home. When she thought of those dreadful few minutes she tried not to hate him, but it became more difficult as her conviction that he did remember but had chosen not to, grew stronger.

She recalled his questions—*"Have you been here all night?", "Was it very uncomfortable sleeping in the chair?"*—underlining the fact that he had no memory of the night's events. Had they underlined it a little too determinedly? She had thought so then, but now, with the hard-won wisdom of a few more years, she saw that they could have meant the opposite, that he might have half remembered and been trying to prompt her into telling him.

She hadn't seen him again. He'd called to say he'd passed the exams well, "Thanks to you," but he hadn't suggested an evening out to celebrate. With his excellent qualifications he was going to London to try his luck.

"That's a long way," she faltered, dismayed.

"It's where the money is," he'd said briskly. "By the way, I owe you five pounds."

"It doesn't matter."

"Of course it does. I'll put it in the mail to you."

"Thank you," she'd said blankly.

He'd sent her the check before he'd left town. A silence followed, then a letter had arrived from London a few weeks later, thanking her at more length for the part she'd played in his success. By that time she'd known she was pregnant, and she'd studied every word of the letter, frantic to find some hint that he missed her. But it was calm, polite and curiously stilted, the letter of a man who had nothing to say. Bitterly she'd wondered why he'd bothered to write at all.

And now that it was too late she saw clearly why he'd bothered. He'd been sending her his new address, hoping she would use it.

Twice Jordan had reached out pleading hands to her, in the clumsy, uncertain gestures of a man who'd never known human warmth. And twice she'd turned her back on him.

His words came back to her, "easy to talk when you've had everything... you dare to blame me because I'm poor... *you've had everything... I'm poor...*"

She'd denied him his child, telling herself that she was too proud to trouble a man who didn't want her. But now, in the harsh light of self-condemnation that she turned on her own motives, her pride took on an uglier aspect. The truth was that she'd been punishing him for not loving her enough, never thinking that one day they would meet again, and she would be forced to confront the devastation that punishment had inflicted on him.

"Hey!" Rick called indignantly.

Startled, Veronica came back to the present and realized she was in Rick's studio, posing in jeans. "What's the matter?" she asked, dazed.

"You're the matter. This is a photo session. You can't sit there crying like that."

Chapter Twelve

Kate Adams had her back to the door when it opened and she heard someone say, "I'd like to see Mr. Cavendish please."

"Do you have an appointment?" Kate asked automatically as she turned. Then she saw who it was and immediately said, "Wait here a moment." She opened Jordan's door and said, "Miss Grant is here."

He looked up with a painful eagerness in his dark eyes, but the next moment it had changed to astonishment. "Holly!" he exclaimed. "What are you doing here? Is... is your mother with you?"

Holly shook her head. "I wanted to see you alone," she said simply.

Jordan came swiftly around to the front of his desk. "Kate, we're not to be disturbed for any reason," he commanded. "No calls, no visitors, nothing."

When the door had closed he sat down on a leather sofa and took Holly's hands in his, gazing lovingly at her face as though he was afraid she would vanish. She studied him in return. "You don't look too good," she said sympathetically.

He looked terrible. Since the day when the three of them had been together in this office he'd eaten little and hardly slept at all. This much Holly's shrewd young eyes could see. What she was too inexperienced to guess was that he'd started drinking heavily. This morning his grooming was as immaculate as ever, but his eyes were sunken, with dark smudges beneath them, and his face was too pale.

He was living at the extreme edge of his nerves, and for the past few days his staff had crept around on tiptoe, but it would never have occurred to Holly to be in awe of Jordan, and she promptly put her arms around his neck and hugged him. The spontaneous sympathy in that action brought him even closer to the breaking point than the glare of accusation she'd flung at him at their last meeting, and he held her tightly against him, unable to say a word.

After a long moment they pulled apart and Holly brushed a lock of hair back from his forehead. "Does your mother know you're here?" he asked.

"No, Mommy's at work. I go to stay with Mrs. Carter in the apartment above while she's out, but I slipped out to see you."

"That was nice of you. I was afraid we were no longer friends, and I'd have hated that."

Holly nodded. "You're my *best* friend," she said simply, and felt her hand squeezed in a firm grip that said more than words. "I miss you," she confided. "I use my computer all the time, and pretend you're there, but it isn't the same."

"I miss you, too. I'm glad you haven't forgotten me."

"Aren't you coming back anymore? You said you had plans, and that we'd be seeing more of each other."

"I know. But since then things have changed. I'm not sure what went wrong, but your mother..." He hesitated, not wanting to confuse Holly by seeming to blame Veronica. "I don't think she likes me now," he finished guardedly.

"Is that because of Mrs. Haslam?" Holly asked.

"Mrs. Haslam? What does she have to do with anything?"

"I mean, after Mommy found out you went to meet her on my birthday—"

"What are you talking about, Holly? I didn't go to meet her. I went because Kate called to say the takeover I was arranging had started to fall through." He saw her looking at him dubiously. "What gave you the idea I went to meet Mrs. Haslam?"

"Because she called after you'd gone and said so."

"What?" Jordan drew back to see Holly's face. Then he gently pulled her down onto the sofa beside him. "I want you to tell me everything," he said.

"She called and asked to speak to you. Mommy said you'd gone, and she said you'd be early for your date with her. And then—" Holly's brow wrinkled with the effort of memory "—she said something about her and Mommy having to be understanding about each other, and she was prepared to make allowances for a while—what was that you said?"

"Nothing," Jordan said hastily, swallowing the curse he'd muttered under his breath. "What else can you remember?"

"Not very much. She was terribly rude to Mommy. She accused her of playing her cards cleverly. And there was something about Mrs. Haslam's husbands. I couldn't quite follow that bit, but Mommy was ever so mad by then and she gave as good as she got. Mrs. Haslam said her husbands were always rich because she used her intelligence and Mommy said she doubted her intelligence had anything to do with it."

Despite himself Jordan's lips twitched. "Did she really say that?"

"Mommy's a good fighter when she's mad," Holly said proudly.

"Yes, I know. But Holly, whatever Mrs. Haslam may have said, I didn't go to meet her. In fact, I'd said a final goodbye to her that day we all met at the Ritz. I promise you that's true. Do you believe me?"

"Of course," Holly declared, looking slightly shocked. "But Mommy doesn't know that."

"Mrs. Haslam must have called me, and when she found I wasn't there she took the chance to leave a false impression."

"Why did she do that?"

"Because she's an opportunist. Do you know what that is?"

Holly nodded. "You told me: someone who makes people kick themselves for not thinking of it first."

"I was talking about business," Jordan said hastily. "This is a different kind of opportunist. She was trying to make trouble between your mother and me. Now I see why—" He checked himself. He saw why Lorrayne had started calling him persistently, refusing to be deterred by rebuffs, but he didn't complete the sentence because despite her air of wisdom Holly was only nine years old. "How do you come to know so much about what Mrs. Haslam said?" he asked.

"I was listening on the extension," Holly confessed, adding quickly, "like you told me to."

"*I* told you to eavesdrop on other people's phone calls?"

"Not quite in those words," Holly conceded, "but you said if I'd set my heart on something, good intelligence work was vital."

He looked at her eagerly. "What is it you've set your heart on?"

Holly shook her head. "I'm playing my cards close to my chest," she said firmly.

"You're quite right," he said. "It's just that... it would help if you could tell me where I stand. I'm confused."

The discovery of how Lorrayne had misled Veronica had given him a moment's hope, but he knew it wasn't the final answer. "You see," he went on, half to her, half to himself. "I did everything wrong."

"When was that?"

"From start to finish. But mostly the other day, when you and your mother were here, I said things I shouldn't have and I didn't say what I really meant. In business it's easy. If something isn't working out, you simply decide where you're going wrong and take steps to get yourself back on track. But it doesn't work with people. That day I knew I was getting it all wrong, and it didn't help. The more I tried the worse it became. Now I'm just confused."

"I'm confused, too," Holly said unexpectedly. "That's why I came here, because only you can tell me."

"Tell you what?"

She took a deep breath. "I came to ask you if you're my father."

The photo session seemed to stretch on for all eternity, but at last Rick said, "Right, that's it!" and Veronica was free to go. She changed hurriedly, but before leaving she called to ask about Holly, as she always did. But as soon as Mrs. Carter came on the line she knew something was badly wrong.

"I'm so glad you called," Mrs. Carter wailed. "Holly's vanished."

Veronica's heart plummeted sickeningly. "What do you mean? How could she vanish?" she managed to say.

"She slipped out while I was in the kitchen. I came back into the living room to find a note pinned to a cushion. It says 'I'm ever so sorry, but I had to go out for a while. If Mommy calls, tell her I'm all right and I'll be home soon. Holly.' I've been wondering what to do. Shall I call the police?"

Veronica's heart steadied. "No, there's no need," she said. "I think I know where she's gone. Don't worry."

She hung up and dialed Jordan's office. In a strange way she wasn't surprised. Holly had been unusually quiet since she'd last seen him, but she'd been so preoccupied with her own unhappiness that she hadn't paid enough attention.

At last she got through. "Kate, I'd like to speak to Mr. Cavendish."

"I'm sorry, he's not speaking to anyone just now."

"But it's urgent. I've got to speak to him."

"I'm really sorry, but I've had orders to allow no calls and no visitors."

"But...Kate, have you seen Holly this afternoon?"

"Oh, yes, she came to see Mr. Cavendish. Hello? Hello?"

Kate was talking to empty air. Veronica had dropped the receiver and rushed out into the street. Nameless fears were shrieking inside her head. Jordan had done this. Somehow he'd persuaded Holly to go to him, and then he planned to spirit her away. She could be out of the country by now.

She reached the headquarters of Cavendish Holdings and tore inside. At the top floor she ran out of the elevator and straight across the lobby to throw open Jordan's door.

And then she stopped.

"Hello, Mommy," Holly said.

Veronica hardly heard. She was looking at the man who rose, his gaze fixed on her, and she knew at once that her suspicions of him had been unworthy. His haggard face revealed everything he'd never been able to say, and her heart ached with love and regret for what she'd done to him.

There was a terrible hope in Jordan's voice as he said, "Holly has just asked me if I'm her father. But I haven't answered her."

Veronica looked at the little girl and saw the same desperate hope reflected in her eyes. "Yes," she said gently. "This is your father."

She waited for the look of joy she knew would pass between the two who'd found each other at last, but neither of them took their eyes off her. Like a man in a dream Jordan walked toward her, moving slowly, as though with each step he expected a rebuff. Suddenly nothing mattered but to ease the pain she'd given him.

She opened her arms, and he came home to them. They stood holding each other, until at the same moment they each put an arm out to draw Holly into the circle.

The little girl hugged them both joyfully, then some instinctive wisdom prompted her to break away and move to the door. But before leaving she said, "It's all right, Mommy. That lady was just an opportunist." Then she slipped out quickly.

As soon as the door closed Jordan and Veronica were in each other's arms again. Veronica felt all Jordan's unspoken love in his kiss, and her fears fell away from her. Explanations could come later. All that mattered now was that they were together. He held her tightly, hardly able to believe that the woman who'd refused him bitterly the other day had finally gathered him so eagerly to her heart.

After a while Veronica managed to speak, and she said the thing she thought he most wanted to hear. "Holly's yours, I promise you. I'll never try to keep you apart."

But he shook his head. "Are *you* mine?" he asked huskily. "That's what I have to know."

"I've always been yours, my darling. I was yours long ago. I'll be yours until the end of my life."

"We made love that night, didn't we? In the morning, all I remembered was a dream, but it was the most beautiful dream of my life, and I longed for it to be real because it would have meant you loved me. If you'd told me, I could have found a way to let you know what you were to me, and I'd never have let you go. I always loved you, Ronnie, but I didn't know how to say so. All I could do was talk a lot of foolishness about detachment and traveling faster alone, but the love was there, if you could only have seen it.

"After I went away I used to look at the mail every day, but I knew you wouldn't write. You'd let me go so cheerfully, as though I was nothing to you. And when I remembered how I'd made love with you in my dreams, I didn't know how to face you."

"But I thought you didn't care for me. Oh, Jordan, I've been blind for a long time, but today I finally saw. Rick told me how you forced him to give up the Jezebel pictures. It made me think, and I saw things I should have seen long ago. If this hadn't happened I was coming to you, anyway, to beg your forgiveness."

"You... want *my* forgiveness?" he echoed, as if he couldn't understand the words.

"Yes—for everything, for keeping Holly from you, for all the years we lost. I told myself I was doing the right thing, but I harmed both of you. You two need each other. I've known that from the first moment you met, but I was terrified that you might try to take her from me."

"You accused me of meaning to marry you only to divorce you... because of Lorrayne? My darling, I've never lied to you. It's over with Lorrayne. After my first visit to Elmbridge I did some thinking, too. I knew I had to fight to win you all over again from the beginning. I called Lorrayne and arranged a meeting to tell her it was over between us. I picked the Ritz because a public place seemed safer. But by ill luck you met, and when she saw you and Holly she must have put two and two together. I didn't go to meet her on Holly's birthday. She called hoping to find a way to make trouble, and she found it."

"How do you know she called?"

"Because our daughter was listening in on the extension."

"Oh, no," Veronica gasped. "And she's kept it to herself all this time?"

"Well, she believes in playing her cards close to her chest," Jordan said with a grin. "She's a real chip off the old block. You're going to have trouble with both of us when we're married."

"Married?"

"We're getting married as soon as I can fix it—" He stopped himself with an appalled look. "I mean, *please*, darling, marry me."

"Mr. Fixit," she teased with a shaky laugh.

"If you marry me I'll change. I swear I'll change."

She kissed him tenderly. "No, you won't."

"No, I don't suppose I will," he admitted. "I made a mess of it when I asked you to marry me the first time. I don't love you because of Holly. I love her because of you, because we created her together, from our love. Promise to marry me."

"I'll marry you. Holly would never forgive me if I didn't." But she saw his face and became serious again. "I'll marry you, Jordan, because I love you. I've never loved anyone but you. I never will."

His mouth covered hers in a kiss in which tenderness and passion mixed with promise for the future that had been given back to them. It might be a stormy future because they were both strong-willed and proud, but they would survive together because the love that united them was built on the lessons of the past.

Neither of them heard the door open just wide enough for a small head to appear and then close again very, very carefully.

* * * * *

COMING NEXT MONTH

#598 VALLEY OF RAINBOWS—Rita Rainville
Liann Murphy respected the mysteries of Hawaii's past while Cody Hunter understood the promises of its future. Could they build their dream together in the magical valley of rainbows?

#599 SIMPLY SAM—Deana Brauer
For years Jake Silvercloud had known Samantha Smith as "tagalong" tomboy Sam, but she'd grown up—with a vengeance—and Sam was ready to lead the handsome rancher on a merry, loving chase....

#600 TAKING SAVANAH—Pepper Adams
Her former husband, Beau, had knocked Southern belle Savanah Winslow off her feet with the news that they were still married. Could she resist giving the brash Yankee another chance?

#601 THE BLAKEMORE TOUCH—Diana Reep
As his public relations consultant, Christina Hayward had to preserve Marc Blakemore's glittering image—and maintain a professional distance. But Marc's masterful touch was getting a firm grip on her heart....

#602 HOME AGAIN—Glenda Sands
Nicki Fox's high-school crush on Kenneth Blackwell had meant nothing—until she went back home and found herself working with him. Now old feelings were becoming a very adult chemistry....

#603 ANY SUNDAY—Debbie Macomber
Marjorie Majors was never squeamish—unless she got ill. Dr. Sam Bretton had allayed her fears with his charming bedside manner, and now Marjorie needed his *loving* care...forever.

AVAILABLE THIS MONTH:

#592 JUSTIN—Book 2 of the LONG, TALL TEXANS trilogy
Diana Palmer

#593 SHERLOCK'S HOME
Sharon De Vita

#594 FINISHING TOUCH
Jane Bierce

#595 THE LADYBUG LADY
Pamela Toth

#596 A NIGHT OF PASSION
Lucy Gordon

#597 THE KISS OF A STRANGER
Brittany Young

ATTRACTIVE, SPACE SAVING BOOK RACK

Display your most prized novels on this handsome and sturdy book rack. The hand-rubbed walnut finish will blend into your library decor with quiet elegance, providing a practical organizer for your favorite hard-or soft-covered books.

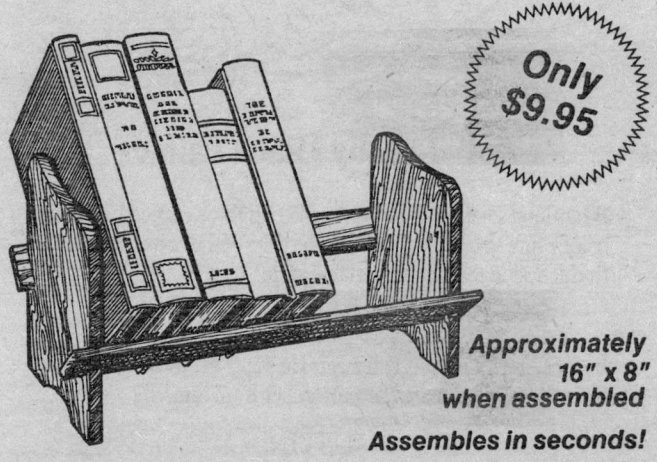

Only $9.95

Approximately 16" x 8" when assembled

Assembles in seconds!

To order, rush your name, address and zip code, along with a check or money order for $10.70* ($9.95 plus 75¢ postage and handling) payable to *Silhouette Books*.

Silhouette Books
Book Rack Offer
901 Fuhrmann Blvd.
P.O. Box 1396
Buffalo, NY 14269-1396

Offer not available in Canada.

*New York and Iowa residents add appropriate sales tax.

A Trilogy by Diana Palmer

Bestselling Diana Palmer has rustled up three rugged heroes in a trilogy sure to lasso your heart! The titles of the books are your introduction to these unforgettable men:

CALHOUN

In June, meet Calhoun Ballenger. He wants to protect Abby Clark from the world, but can he protect her from himself?

JUSTIN

Calhoun's brother, Justin—the strong, silent type—has a second chance with the woman of his dreams, Shelby Jacobs, in August.

TYLER

October's long, tall Texan is Shelby's virile brother, Tyler, who teaches shy Nell Regan to trust her instincts—especially when they lead her into his arms!

Don't miss CALHOUN, JUSTIN and TYLER—three gripping new stories coming soon from Silhouette Romance!

SRLTT